STEELDUST II
—The Flight

BY J.P.S. BROWN

**Steeldust
Jim Kane
The Outfit
The Forests Of The Night**

STEELDUST II
—*The Flight*

J.P.S. Brown

Walker and Company
New York

First published in the United States of America in 1987 by the Walker Publishing Company, Inc.

Published simultaneously in Canada by John Wiley & Sons Canada, Limited, Rexdale, Ontario.

Library of Congress Cataloging-in-Publication Data

Brown, J.P.S.
  Steeldust II—the flight.

  I. Title.   II. Title: Steeldust 2—the flight.
III. Title: Steeldust two—the flight.
PS3552,R6856S75 1987   813'.54   86–26654
ISBN 0–8027–0944–3

Printed in the United States of America

10   9   8   7   6   5   4   3   2   1

This book is for Natalia Shane, my godmother, who healed me, hugged me, and fed me albondigas.

PREFACE

The old rancher came in from the pasture one day, angry because his son was not out in the corral working with his colts, and caught the boy reading a book.

"What're you doing?" he asked.

"Oh, just reading," said the son.

"What're you reading?"

"The Book of Knowledge."

"A book of knowledge, huh? Well, if you really want to know something, I'll give you one of those colts out there, any one you want. You raise him, train him, use him, give him all the care he needs every day, and keep him all his life. That way you'll be able to keep going on about your business, and you won't have to stop and read a book when you want to know something. Now, get a movin'."

STEELDUST II
—*The Flight*

CHAPTER 1

The Mexicans believe a wistful devil will often visit a good horse at night. When a man discovers tresses twisted in his horse's mane, it means the horse has been visited by the devil. The devil might not be able to corrupt a good horse the way he can a good man, but he can leave tresses in his mane to show he covets him.

BILL Shane and Tom Ford were headed for town, as soon as they reported to their boss. They had been on the trail six weeks, sleeping under their tarps with rocks in their beds, eating dust off the heels of thirty-six hundred cows, bathing in mud tanks when they could find water enough to swim a toad. Now they were headed for the shade to submerge their hides in clear hot water, drink cold beer, swallow whiskey, and turn themselves loose to run and play.

The herd was between Red Rock and the Roblez Ranch by Tucson, making five miles a day and headed for Port Libertad on the Mexican Sea of Cortez. It would pasture on Indian wheat through the winter and spring, along the coastal desert of Sonora.

Bill and Tom had not taken their turn in town yet, and they would not likely have another chance to go until they brought the herd back from Mexico. They would not find Canadian whiskey in Mexico. Bill could get it at the Blue Moon Club in the Pioneer Hotel in Tucson, even though Prohibition was in force. He could buy mescal on any street corner. The year was 1926 and the mescal routes were established by the smugglers who brought it muleback from

1

Sonora. The *mezcaleros* of Sonora sold more mescal in Arizona than they did in the whole republic of Mexico.

Bill loved to drink that Canadian whiskey in town, when he could get it. He worked hard and that made him streamlined. But being streamlined didn't mean a thing if a man couldn't get out and turn himself loose and celebrate being back among humans once in awhile.

The man who owned the herd, the High Lonesome Ranch, and the Red Rock Ranch was R.E. Bradford. Bill was his foreman and Tom his cowboss. Bill, Tom, and a crew had just driven the High Lonesome herd from its headquarters in Apache County to the desert. R.E. had summoned them to his house in Red Rock this morning.

The cowboys were lighthearted as they left their horses in the corral and tramped over R.E.'s back porch. Mrs. Bradford welcomed them into her kitchen, and their outlook improved even more when she gave them coffee in china cups, a pitcher of fresh cream, and a plate of light bread. She put out silver spoons and napkins for them. Mrs. Bradford was a nice, gentle lady, but she was usually cool to her cowboys. Bill and Tom were sitting at her kitchen table recalling their manners and happy they had not forgotten to wash and shave before they left their wagon, when R.E. came looking for them. They put their cups back in the saucers and followed him to his office.

Bill had hoped to see Mary, R.E.'s daughter, while he was there. He had thought she might have heard he was coming and would be outside to greet him, but he did not see her, and he heard no sound of her as he walked through the house. When he and Tom sat down in the office to do business with R.E. Bill was still watching and listening for her. Lately, Bill had discovered a terrible passion for Mary, and it had caught him by surprise. She had been a gangly little girl when Bill started working for R.E. Then one day about six months ago, a good looking young woman walked up to him and smiled—she was Mary.

She had grown up showing a lot of good style and Bill had been in on her training. He liked helping a young horse, or a young person grow up and amount to something. Mary had always taken an interest in ranch work and was a natural with horses. She was smart in school and popular with local society. Bill had figured she would grow up, marry a banker, and hire men like Bill to saddle her horse when she wanted to go out horseback riding before cocktails with her friends.

As far as Bill was concerned, about the only thing a cowpuncher had was his freedom. The worst that could happen to him would be to discover he had a passion that would make him give up his freedom for one female, but Bill decided he was ready to give it away when the young woman walked up and smiled at him a few months ago.

"The herd came through the drive in better shape than I expected," R.E. was saying. "We still own it and we marketed the steers, even though we had to cram them down our banker's throat. For a time I stood to lose my herd. You men saved it for me and I'm thankful to you. As long as I have land and livestock, you two have a home and a place to work."

Bill thought: Yes, we saved your money, but Jonas Ryan got killed. And the crew could use the rest of its wages, but what the hell, why remind you? The crew was only paid a third of its wages when the herd arrived at Red Rock because R.E. had his tail caught in the door of his banker's vault.

Jonas was a Texas cowboy who had joined the High Lonesome crew when the drive began. Right after the herd crossed the Gila River a dust storm turned it back. Bill sent Jonas back to help hold the cattle on the Gila. On his way, Jonas caught a bunch of Yaquis driving away eleven big steers. He was riding a counterfeit bronc named Copper, and when he tried to take the cattle back from the Yaquis, Copper fell on him and killed him.

After Copper was found Bill cut him loose from the remuda to shift for himself on the desert. As far as Bill was concerned, the horse had a notch in his tail because he had killed a man.

Bill figured R.E. should not be complaining about forcing the banker to buy the steers. Richard Claire, the banker, had laid a trap for R.E. and had tried to foreclose on his herd when it reached Red Rock. Bill made him take the steers in payment of his lien. At that time Bill thought he was cramming the steers down Claire's throat because he did not know that the drought-weakened cattle-market had come back to life while the herd was on the trail from the High Lonesome. The herd was worth a lot more money at the end of the drive than it had been at the start. The only complaint Claire could have was that Bill had not let him take R.E.'s entire herd for the money that was owed him.

". . . We'll survive if it rains and the market stays alive so we can sell our steer calves in May," R.E. was saying. "We've been dry too long and fat cattle are scarce. Maybe our steers will be in good flesh when you bring them back from the Mexican coast. Don't wait until you run out of feed to start back. Now, if you can keep the crew together until you move the herd away from town, I'll feel lucky.

"I think everything is working out for us, after all. We haven't lost our banker like I thought we had—Claire came to see me yesterday evening and we've decided to go on doing business with one another. In fact, we're traveling together with our wives to the National Livestock Exposition in Chicago."

R.E. looked closely at Bill. Bill crossed one leg over the other and looked at his boot.

"I know you fellers don't think much of Claire," R.E. said. "Business yokes strange oxen together. I can do Claire's bank a lot of good, and he doesn't want to hurt his position in the community by making an enemy of me. He's financing other cattlemen in the state and he can't afford to stay mad at me. He's making his bank's money available to me, and I've decided to forget the way he tried to take my herd. He fired Lindano, that foreman of his. He claims Lindano acted out of pure hatred of you, Bill, when he caused trouble on the drive."

R.E. stood up, walked to the front of his desk and sat on the edge. He told them, "So, everything turned out all right in spite of Bill's manhandling of Claire and Lindano. I'm lucky Claire was man enough to come back and talk it over. He needs me, and I need him, and that's settled. You're lucky I need you, Bill, because if I didn't, you'd be in jail. Think about that the next time you feel like kicking the chair out from under a man like Claire. You've made an enemy for life there. If you ever tried to go into business for yourself, you'd have a hard time getting by that man. You're probably not a bit worried about business and I envy you. Sometimes I feel like leaving town and going out and cowboying with you fellers without a worry, but I can't.

"Bill, you never told me you and Lindano had it in for each other. What caused all that?"

"Lindano went on the drive we made two years ago. He lost cattle on the trail, and we paid him to go back and bring them in. He showed up regularly for his pay, but never brought in the cattle. He and I had words about that and since then we've never been able to get along. I hate the way he treats horses; He beats them and uses a quirt made of rawhide woven over a chain. He's a thief and knows I have him pegged. He covets everything he sees and is jealous of any man who rides good horses, because he can't teach a horse anything himself or make a good hand horseback. But most of all—I can't prove it—I know he followed the same cattle Jonas tried to get back from the Yaquis when he got killed. I saw him leave the herd to bring those same cattle back in the storm. I'm almost sure he drove those cattle off the herd to give them to the Yaquis and cause us trouble. We never saw him again on the trail after Jonas got killed; Lindano quit us right after the storm. He came in to Red

Rock and joined Claire before we came in with the herd. I know he's responsible for Jonas's death."

"You mean you suspect that he is responsible. You don't know. Your suspicions are not reason for hitting him in the face with your spurs the way you did. You could go to the pen for that."

"I hope I harelipped him. I'll give him worse treatment the next time he comes near a herd I'm trying to move."

"I don't approve of the way you handled that. Or the business with Claire. However, it seems you're going to get away with it, after all. No charges have been filed against you."

Bill was thinking R.E. sure was an old hypocrite. R.E. had practically sicked him on the banker. Claire had been cheating R.E., not Bill. Bill had put a scare into the banker to convince him he did not need to take R.E.'s whole herd to satisfy his lien. Bill had put himself in danger of going to jail for R.E.'s sake, not his own. Bill just spread the banker out on the floor without harming him, and the banker had consented to take the steers before Bill could really hurt him.

"Anyway, business is business," R.E. was saying. "Claire is extending me unlimited credit, and a man in the cow business always needs credit. Besides, my wife and Claire's wife are friends. Mary and Tony, Claire's son, have always been good friends. Tony is strong and honest and his friendship with Mary will probably grow even more. We'll be seeing Claire and his family socially for a long time."

Bill looked into R.E.'s cold eyes. He could see the man was banking on his daughter. Her friendship with Tony Claire meant money to R.E., and Bill was being told to recognize and respect it as good business practice. R.E. had already ordered Bill to stay away from Mary once when he realized Bill was showing too much interest in her. Bill relaxed and smiled to himself.

Tony Claire was a big, green, gunsel kid, in love with his

muscles. He had grown up with Mary and had started dating her. Bill got to know Tony when the kid signed on to ride with the High Lonesome crew on the drive because his father wanted him to learn the cattle business. Tony Claire and Bill did not like each other at first. Gradually, though, because of all the troubles that happen to a greenhorn on the trail, Tony began trying to make a hand. He and Bill settled their differences when they reached Red Rock, and Tony decided to go on with the herd to Mexico.

Bill turned his attention to R.E. The man sometimes acted as though he had a warm heart, but his eyes were always cold. He was a fair boss; always fair, always boss. He paid well for services, but he sure got his money's worth out of a cowboy.

R.E. saw that Bill understood him, so he turned and addressed his business to Tom. While they were talking, Bill walked to the window and looked outside. He belonged outside. As soon as he could get going without acting insulted, he left the house through the kitchen.

Mrs. Bradford smiled kindly and coolly at him. Bill could see she knew all about the message R.E. had given him and expected him to take himself on out of sight without pause.

Bill saddled Lizard and waited. He saw Tom sitting at the kitchen table chatting with R.E. and Mrs. Bradford. Bill never understood how Tom could be so at ease with them. He just sat and visited and enjoyed them, and they seemed to enjoy him. But Mrs. Bradford always looked at Bill the way she looked at her racehorse. Feed him, keep him good looking, run the hell out of him, brag on him, let someone else claim him before all the new wore off him—and then remember him fondly.

Bill walked over to Steeldust's stall. The horse looked up to see if Bill was carrying something for him to eat. His back was clean and dry, and his barrel was full to popping. The Devil's tresses were tangling his mane because Mary had not been out to brush him. He had everything else he needed, though. Bill's top horse in the boss's best stall was as close as Bill Shane would ever come to the Bradford meal and straw, and that was the damned truth.

About the second worst passion a cowpuncher could discover in himself was a passion for one horse. Just about the time Bill had discovered a passion for Mary, he realized he had to have Steeldust, this stud colt. Bill had named him after the colt's famous ancestor, Steel Dust, who was the great sire of a line of horses that cowboys in the Southwest liked best.

Steeldust was the best horse Bill had ever ridden, and Bill had a reputation for being a good hand with a horse. The colt had quickly learned the difference between turning cattle back and running them away. At a dead run, Bill could rein him in and roll him back in his tracks just by speaking to him and touching his rein; when Steeldust had cattle in front of him, he made them do what he wanted them to do. He had an easy, ground-eating foxtrot that kept Bill rested on long circles. He handled a rope well, and he was fast and catty on his feet. Besides all that, he had a fine luster in his eye.

At the end of the drive to Red Rock, Mary talked Bill into letting her keep Steeldust so she could feed and rest him. Now the colt was in horse heaven. He was where Bill would like to be—with Mary petting him, making over him, and spoiling him into a state of complete worthlessness. Which just proved that a top horse often made his own best deals.

Later, when Bill and Tom were headed for town, Tom said, "You're going to Mary's fashion show tonight, aren't you, Salty Bill?"

"What show is that?"

"Mrs. Bradford invited us to a fashion ball at the Pioneer Hotel. The stores are putting it on. Mary's modeling a Goldwater gown. Mrs. Bradford told me to be sure you went."

Bill stood in his stirrups, took off his hat, held it over his breast, and gazed back at the Bradford house from over the top of his nose. "Lordy, Lord," he said.

"Does that mean Mary didn't tell you about the fashion ball? You mean you're not invited, Bill?"

"Oh, I'm invited," said Bill. "I just don't know if I can make it. I haven't had time to order my tuxedo."

"You have to learn to socialize, you know."

"Now, ain't that a helluva deal?" Bill said.

In town, Bill and Tom refitted with new hats, shirts, boots and Levis. They bought tobacco and stowed it away safely so they would have it if they spent all their money on whiskey before they headed back to the herd.

At noon, they headed for the Pioneer Hotel, where cowmen and cowboys congregated. They registered and walked onto the elevator with the other humans. Bill and Tom seemed unconscious of the smell of cattle dust, horse manure, work sweat, and camp smoke they brought to closed places. They looked away unconcerned as their neighbors inside the elevator were forced to endure their presence while coping with the danger of rising in this contraption to the upper stories.

The two men politely held their hats on their chests and watched the numbers of the floors change over the door. They glanced at their neighbors' faces as they stepped out. They sighed with relief at freeing their odors from the distressful place. They carried their carcasses quickly away to the room and the bath without saying a word about how each noticed the other smelled too strong all of a sudden. They bathed, and shaved, and changed into their new clothes.

Bill wore his beaded moccasins that a Bannock Indian girl had made him a long time ago when he had gone to another town to drink whiskey. The moccasins were his only clothes that still smelled of camp smoke because they had been tanned in smoke.

Bill and Tom headed for the Blue Moon, a club that had its rooms by the Pioneer Hotel lobby. The place served soft drinks and setups, and was a popular speakeasy for the lawless drinkers of Tucson during Prohibition. The chief of police was the Blue Moon's best customer, people said.

The club was crowded with cowmen and their lady friends. By late afternoon everyone was wearing his hat cocked on the side of his head and was talking big. Tom matched Bill against a young cattle trader named Jimmy Morrow in a chair-jumping contest. The match did not require that Jimmy jump a chair at all. Tom bet him that Bill could stand flatfooted behind the high back of an ordinary chair, jump and clear the back with both feet, and sit in the chair.

Bill said, "Tom, I've never jumped over a chair like that."

"I didn't bet you'd done it. I bet you could do it," said Tom. "I know you can do it. Concentrate. Do it, or we've given Morrow fifty dollars."

"I've never used my feet for jumping over chairs."

"Never mind. I know you can do it because you've got on your moccasins. I saw those moccasins just fly in Blackfoot, Idaho."

Bill walked up behind the chair, stopped, jumped over the back, and sat in the chair without touching it with anything but his butt. Tom picked up his winnings.

"All right," said Jimmy, unfolding more banknotes. "How many chairs can he jump?"

Tom announced, "We can broad jump ten such chairs placed side by side."

"Tom, I don't want to jump chairs," said Bill. "I came here to drink whiskey. We're going to have to go back to the herd early because you're wild to gamble away all our money. And what if I break a leg? That floor is hard."

"Believe me, you can't hurt yourself. Don't touch the floor. Fly over ten chairs and they'll give up." Tom began lining up the chairs.

Bill walked toward the lobby to make his run. The crowd in the club was making bets. A heavy, clean-shaven man in a dark corner was betting on Bill and calling all bets. The man seemed familiar, but Bill did not have time to think about him. He made a run at the chairs, jumped them, and slammed through a door into the street.

Jimmy yelled, "Any eighth-grade schoolboy can do that, I bet two hundred dollars he can't jump fifteen chairs."

"We'll bet two hundred dollars against five hundred dollars," Tom said, as Bill came in from the street.

"We haven't got two hundred dollars to bet," Bill said. "I ain't betting my horse money."

"Just dig up some of that Lindano money you won for us cutting cattle," said Tom. "I ain't putting up *all* the money. What if you can't jump fifteen chairs?"

"Us? Us? It's funny to me it's *us's* money you're betting now that your big mouth made an impossible bet. Anyway, I still don't know what *I'm* getting out of all this."

"You get the glory if you do it, or the shame if you don't. What the hell, you don't expect me to take all the loss if you can't jump a few chairs, do you?"

"Nobody can jump fifteen chairs."

"I bet two hundred dollars against five hundred dollars my man can clear fifteen chairs and go out the door on his feet," Tom announced.

"Called. That bet is called," Jimmy shouted.

"Now, dammit, Tom, I barely cleared ten chairs," Bill said.

"Too late for you to back out. Get a better run at it. You can do it, Salty Bill. You *have* to do it. Do you know how long I'd have to work to make five hundred dollars? It's my lifetime dream to own one five hundred-dollar bundle of cash. Jump this little line of chairs and I'll be on my way to becoming a cattle baron just like R.E."

Tom lined up the chairs. Bill walked out into the lobby. The bellboys were making a runway of tables in the center of the lobby for the fashion show. Townspeople were arriving and taking seats, spiking their punch, and building their appetites for a good time. Fancy-looking women, all dressed up, arrived with smiles on their faces and work-ox husbands on their arms. Other women came in coveys with no men to escort them. These women were sincerely interested in fashion and the society of other women. Well-dressed boys, escorting pretty girls their own age, smiled as they walked into the place. Everyone in the lobby was being nice.

Bill could see the heavy, clean-shaven man snatching bet money over his head in his dark corner of the club. He was wearing a new hat. Bill gave him time to cover all bets and then launched himself at the chairs again. He let himself fly and landed running on the other side of the fifteenth chair. He hit the door just as two well-dressed couples were coming in off the street—Tony Claire with Mary, and his father and mother. Bill hit the door just as the elder Claire was reaching for the handle outside. Bill went through the people like a cue ball through the stripes, scattering them over the sidewalk. Tony's mother shrieked and kept her feet, though she held on to Claire's hand when he sprawled on his back. Tony and Mary bounded away, kicking up their heels and laughing. Tony saw that his mother was delighted and began laughing with her.

Bill only saw that Mary was parading with his enemy. He had thought Claire was Mary's enemy too. He did not back away from her with apologies for upsetting her entrance to the ball. He felt he had caught her in worse mischief than jumping chairs. The last time Mary had been with the banker, as Bill remembered it, she had been telling Claire how low on the social scale he was.

Bill helped Claire to his feet, while his heart was taking on a load it had been feeling too light to carry. No one had been hurt by the encounter but him. Claire's wife was still laughing because she did not know Bill from a bastard calf. Tony was laughing, too. He was probably just happy to be with Mary, heading for a dance and catching Bill drunk. Tony probably did not know about Bill's most recent differences with his father. But Mary was not amused about being spun on the street in her fashions, and she was no longer laughing. Claire jerked away from Bill when he regained his feet. All four of the people were talking to Bill, each in a different humor, but he had no idea what any of them were saying.

Bill apologized, just as he would to any stranger he might happen to knock down in the street, and he walked back into the club. As she walked through the room, Mary glanced at him as though he were some stranger she was trying to recognize. She looked away when Bill gave her a good look at his face.

The rowdy crowd in the club was anxious for the fashion show to begin. All the well-dressed and jeweled ladies of the town had congregated in the lobby, posing and chatting and calling to one another. They settled their rich bottoms into chairs along the runway so they could watch the models traipse by.

Bill was pounded on the back and congratulated for jumping the chairs and winning the bet. He began to feel better, and he walked out so he could watch the fashion show begin. The heavy man waved at him from his dim corner and sent him a drink. The man was uproarious with drink, and he had plenty of it in plain sight on his table. Various common women with serious eyes and big appetites for drink were sitting around his table. Bill tried to remember him. He was sure he knew the man. How could he not remember him? He had a gap in his grin where an incisor had been. Bill kept thinking he might know him if he were not so clean shaven and wearing a new hat, his face so unblemished. Maybe he was a bootlegger who Bill had never seen sober.

Then, Bill forgot about the man and took up a platter of hors d'oeuvres from a table in the lobby and carried it back into the club. The rounders in the place stripped the platter before he reached his corner. He went back and began carrying hors d'oeuvres until only one platter was left. The people for whom the hors d'oeuvres were intended had not tasted a bite. They were all intent on looking at one another and being looked at. Bill left them one platter; one was enough for the nibbling they would require. The dames all looked well fed and were sitting on expensive fill they had stored from other doings, and he had done them no harm by carrying away their snack.

Feeling rich, happy, popular, and substantially tight with his whiskey, Bill decided to press his luck and put on his own fashion show. He pranced out and posed on the end of the ramp while the ladies applauded. He cavorted down the runway and showed off his new shirt and Levis, his jumping moccasins, and his new drinking hat. He put his hands on his hips, swaggered back, pumped his fists, and bowed. The ladies applauded again, and he laughed and looked right into Mary's offended eyes. She gazed at him as though he were someone she had known when she was doing and saying things too foolish to remember. Bill went back to his place with the rowdies.

The models gathered in the club and waited for their turn to go slinking down the runway. The rounders in the club intimidated them, and they did not look up as they posed and postured and practiced smiles and turns among themselves. The rounders launched each girl with cowboy yells and clapping.

The models returned to the club and one of them sat down by Bill. She told him she was a cowgirl from Cheyenne, in town to attend the university, and she bet she could yell better than he could. She was as pretty as Mary, so Bill began telling her about his horse, Steeldust. She drowned him out with a cowboy yell. Her yell was more musical than Bill's, but not as wild. She began drinking straight shots of whiskey with beer chasers, and her yells became lustier; Bill was certain she would run loose with him at least until dawn. Then, all of a sudden, she stood up to leave.

"Don't go, Cheyenne," Bill pleaded. "Stay and play awhile."

"I just love whiskey and cowboys and a high old time," she said. "But I'm Sheila and I gotta go. See ya."

"Sheila, if you stay, I'll give you my horse, Steeldust," Bill said. He looked over his shoulder and Mary was standing right behind him.

"Oh, so you're trying to woo someone else by giving away your horse," said Mary.

"First come, first served," said Bill. "Or is it, serve the one who best serves you? Tell me the rule you live by, Mary."

"You can't give that horse away. You already gave him to me."

"I just gave him to this Cheyenne cowgirl. As I recall, I told you I'd give him to you when you grew up. Your father ran me off today so you could go on with your girlhood. Now I'm gonna trade that horse for some loving and I ain't gonna wait for you."

Bill turned back to Sheila and saw that all his gift horse had brought him was the sight of her skinny backside headed out the door. He ran to the door in time to see her hurry aboard an open car with other boys and girls her age.

"Come back. Come back, little Sheila," bawled Bill, laughing. He walked back to his place in the club and Mary was still there. "Mary, that was Sheila," he said. "Little lost Sheila from Cheyenne."

"I just wonder how many times you've given that horse away since you came to town," said Mary. She turned away, showed him *her* backside, and walked out. She walked with her head down to hide her eyes from people in a way that broke Bill's drunken heart for one heartbeat. He walked after her to watch her go away and found he was standing by the last tray of hors d'oeuvres. A fashionable lady was discovering them at that moment and was reaching for one with two dainty fingers. Bill picked up the tray.

"Excuse me," said Bill, smiling into the lady's face.

"Oh, I'm so sorry," said the fashion lady. She was an elegant lady, just Bill's age.

"Lady, you look hungry," said Bill. "Come on and I'll feed you."

"Oh, I'm really not hungry," said the fashionable lady, smiling into Bill's face.

"Come on, we're short one fashion lady. I'll give you a sorrel horse."

"All right . . . for a sorrel horse," said the lady playfully.

Late in the night Tom and Bill were at a place called El Charro with the fashion lady. The place was a restaurant and speakeasy. They were sitting on an open patio under a mesquite tree with a gallon jug of mescal. They were drinking mescal with orange juice and ice and listening to a mariachi band. The cool night on Bill's shirt and the mescal warming his skin made him feel supremely satisfied. He looked into the lights of a roadster that pulled up and stopped by the patio. The lights went out, and Mary stepped out of the car and walked toward him. The fashion lady was telling Bill a long story about her divorce while Bill watched Mary walk toward him. He despaired of the lady finishing her tale and leaving before Mary reached him. Mary stopped at the table.

"Hi, Mary," Bill said. He stood up as though he did not care about anyone but her. The fashion lady mewed on about her divorce. Bill moved a chair for Mary. "What brings you to our party?" he asked.

"This looks like the one I've been looking for," Mary said wryly. "I was sure you were headed for a good time and as soon as I could get out of the house I came looking for you."

"That must have been hard for you, Mary, to ditch Tony, your best chum and beau, and sneak away from your daddy's house. Now the cops'll probably come looking for you, find you with us, make us give you up, and maybe take us to jail. Do us a favor. The next time you want adventure, go with Tony. He can get away with keeping you out late."

"You know, looking at it the way you do, I can see I made

a mistake coming here," said Mary. "You're all hooked up with your own brand of fun, and I'm intruding."

"You know how it is when you're out for a good time. With me, it's always first come, first served—after I've been put in my place."

"What's all this about you being put in your place, anyway? Who put you in your place?"

"We had such a nice place, Henry and I," said the fashion lady. "But it *had* to be sold."

"It seems to me you gave up awful easy," said Mary.

"No, it just had to be done," said the fashion lady.

"Gave up, hell. What did I give up?" asked Bill. "You weren't mine to give up. Look at you. You don't belong here. You ought to be in your perfumed little bed, or off smooching in your car with Tony Claire. This lady who has an ex-husband who had to sell her house is my friend, now."

"Is that the way you want it, Bill?"

"No, it's not, but it seems to be the way you and your daddy do, so good luck. You go on with your proms, and your banker beaus, and your growing up and having fun, and I'll go on with old Tom, and mescal, and the herd, taking orders and giving away my horse so I can make out."

"I broke away tonight to give you some loving. Now I find you full of mescal and meanness, and you'd rather see how low you can sink than be with me."

"I'm sorry, Mary. I just couldn't wait. I always do this when I come to town. I can't even be trusted to feed my horse tonight."

Mary stood up. "You think that's it and the only way it's going to be, do you?"

"It looks that way to me."

"Well, I'll show you how it's going to be." Mary began unbuttoning her blouse. She stepped back. "I'll show you." She kicked a shoe at Bill and it buzzed by his ear. Before it came to earth, the other shoe hummed by his other ear. She shed her blouse and threw it in Bill's face.

"Mary, what're you doing?" Bill asked. Mary wheeled and marched away. "Mary, where you going?"

"If a good time is what you want . . ." Mary marched off the crowded patio and across a broad lawn and a park that spread out below the El Charro. She headed for the brush of the desert on the other side of the park, shedding her clothes. A wild crowd on the patio began stamping its feet and clapping and yelling in time to her strides. She was down to her panties and brassiere when she disappeared into the brush.

"My God, a snake'll bite her," said Tom.

"Poor girl," said the fashion lady. "Demented. I know. I know."

"You better go after her, Salty Bill," said Tom. "She needs a hero."

"I'm not going after her," said Bill. "She'll be naked as an infant in two more strides."

"Somebody has to take her clothes to her so she can come back, don't they?" asked Tom.

"You go," said Bill.

Tom trailed Mary into the brush, picking up her clothes. After a while he came back and laid the clothes on the table. "I went as far as I could," he said. "Someone who knows her better'n me has to go the rest of the way. She's down to her panties. Look, here's her *bazeer,* if you don't believe I went as far as a man could go."

Bill spoke gently to the fashion lady and prodded her to see if he could get her to go after Mary. She had laid her head down on the table and was asleep. He stood up. "Where is she?" he asked Tom.

Tom pointed across the park. "She's somewhere on the other side of the big mesquite. You'll find her. She can't go far with no clothes and no shoes. She's already in the cholla."

Bill picked up Mary's clothes and went into the brush and

after a while he saw a silver blur glinting in an open place, by a tall saguaro.

"Dammit, Mary," Bill said. "What the hell do you think you're doing, taking off all your clothes in the middle of town?"

He moved on cautiously and found Mary standing with her head poked into the brush like a wild mare. She straightened and turned to him.

"What are you *doing* there, Mary?" demanded Bill. He was a man easily startled by strange sights in the night. "What do you think you're doing? What if somebody else . . . What if that whole gang had come here looking for you?"

"I don't give a damn," said Mary. "You accused me of being hoity-toity. Now, how do you like me? I didn't come lookin' for you to be ignored, or told how I should act. I came looking for some loving."

Bill walked to her the same way he would walk to a bronc mare, cautious of her overheated condition. She let fly a kick at his head and Bill marveled at the meanness of it. He suspected that if he ever found himself naked in the brush at night, he would be gentle as a white mouse. He was used to heated fillies kicking at his head, though. She kicked again, and he caught hold of her. He thought she would have been slower, more bulky, but her tiny waist fit inside his hands. Her breath was on his face. All his experience with women had been with fat whores and sluggish bawds. Mary was quicksilver. He hugged her until she was still. He stepped away and made her stand while he helped her dress. She stood over him with her head down and her hand on his shoulder, responding like a child, picking up one foot and then the other as she stepped into her clothes. He knelt and put on her shoes. He stuffed her stockings into her pocket, kissed her brow, and led her back toward the patio.

On the way, Bill met the heavy, clean-shaven man with his gang of rowdies coming to see what they could see. The man stepped aside and controlled his crowd while Bill and Mary walked by. Bill still could not remember where he had known the man.

Bill should have asked Mary who the man was. Mary recognized him. The man was Lindano. She wanted to tell Bill, but her pique still had not subsided from the rampage. She knew why Bill did not recognize Lindano. Bill probably did not look closely at the faces of men he disliked. Mary did. Even though she was just a girl, she had the courage to want to know her enemy's face.

This Lindano had caused a lot of trouble on the drive to Red Rock. Lindano, a brand name for a sheep and cattle dip used in Mexico, was also the name of Richard Claire's *pistolero,* a sneak who packed a pistol. Claire had planted him on the drive to keep the herd from arriving at Red Rock with a full count of cattle so Claire would have an excuse to take it over.

Lindano had been Bill's enemy for years and at the end of the drive, Bill finally settled with him. In a fight caused by Lindano's dirty dealings and maltreatment of horses, Bill took his spurs by the straps and brought them down on Lindano's head.

Bill realized everyone had expected him to use a pistol on Lindano. He had a pistol and was a good shot. He had served as a marine in France in the World War.

He did not think of shooting Lindano. Bill did not want to kill him to settle accounts. A man should be able to find some other way.

The reason Bill did not recognize Lindano was he assumed the man's face would be scarred, his lips split by Bill's spurs. He would never have expected to see Lindano clean, smiling, open-handed, and generous, wearing a new hat and having a good time so soon after Bill had taken his spurs to his head. Bill expected Lindano would run and hide at the sight of him. But Mary knew that Lindano had stayed near Bill all day while he was running and playing. Everytime she had seen Bill, she had seen the heavy, clean-shaven man.

The fashion lady had gone away to new adventures when Mary and Bill returned to the patio. Tom handed Mary a full glass of mescal and orange juice and she drank it all. She put down the glass and looked around for more. Bill watched her face. She looked like a colt who had run to the end of her rope as hard as she could, and been jerked down just when she had been sure of getting away. She caught his look and began gazing back at him as steadily as a predator.

Bill began joking with Tom about frenzied mares who ran off in the night, and of the danger of them being caught in barbed wire and scarred for life. Nobody wanted old, scarred and scary, crazy, wire-cut mares. He knew he sounded flippant and Mary was still feeling mean. She kept staring at him.

"It's time to take you home, Mary," Bill said.

"I don't need you to take me home. I brought myself. I can take myself back."

"You need to be safe at home, the way you feel."

"Why should I be safe? Why can you run loose and not me?"

"Because you're too wild to be running loose at night, that's why," Bill said. "I'm taking you home."

He walked her toward her car. Lindano was talking about her, entertaining his gang. The gang was grinning at Mary. The drunks believed they had been given a look at her body, now. The look on Lindano's face was saying he wished his whole gang could know her the way he did. Mary turned and stared at him until he looked away. Bill wanted to load Mary into her car and take her away from the place before she got him into a fight.

"Here, you drive your thing," Bill said, pushing Mary into the car. "My saddle don't fit on it." He cranked the roadster and started it. He climbed in beside Mary and she drove recklessly home.

Every room in R.E.'s townhouse was lit, and all the drapes were drawn. Mary stopped her car, and the curtains in a front room window parted. Mary's mother peered out. Bill walked Mary to the door and turned to leave, but R.E. came out and ordered him inside. Mary's mother looked like a specter as she stepped back into a shadow. Mussed ends of her hair stood away from her wan little face. She was not glad to see Bill.

The townhouse was a mansion where R.E. entertained governors, university presidents and Mexican generals. R.E. was always bragging that he needed an intercom to locate his wife in that house. Shouting would not bring her from even the nearest room. Bill had never been invited to this place.

"Mary, go with your mother," R.E. said. "Bill, walk to my study with me."

"Whatever you have to say to Bill, you can say to me, Daddy," said Mary.

"You're out of this. Go to your mother."

"Daddy, you'll have to whip me to keep me away."

"All right, if you're determined to suffer, come on."

Bill sat down in the study and began rolling a cigarette.

"Now, Mary, let me guess what's been going on," said R.E. "You found Bill drinking with a floozy. He was so drunk his hat was on crooked. That new sack of Bull Durham he just put in his pocket is probably all he's got left to show that he made a payday. What was he drinking? Was he drinking Scotch whisky, or mescal? I'll bet you a new hat he was drinking mescal and didn't give a damn when he saw you coming. Take a good look at him in the light of your home. He's too shabby for you, Mary. I can see it and he can see it; why can't you? What will your life be like if you have to go out every Saturday night and bring Bill home from a saloon?"

Shabby? Bill thought. Shabby is ragged. I'm not shabby. My underwear's clean and my trousers are new and I'm wearing a better hat than any you own, old fart.

"And you, Bill. I know you have to run and play in your own way. I like it. You wouldn't be my kind of man if you didn't have the fun you do. I don't know a better man than you when you're on horseback out in the open. However, when you're afoot in town like everybody else you behave like a team of horses gone wild. You knew I did not want you to become embroiled with Mary."

"I'm not 'embroiled' with Mary."

"Then, what in the hell were you doing out with her at night?"

"Daddy, leave Bill alone," Mary said. "All he did was bring me home."

Bill let R.E. and Mary stare at each other awhile and then he said, "It seems to me you're having fits over nothing, R.E. I'm not interested in seducing your daughter at present, and I'll probably never ask your permission to mate. So, call a truce with her. I'm headed back to the herd. If you're going to fire me, that's just fine, but do it before I hit the door."

Bill stood up to leave.

"Now, Bill, this isn't solving the problem," R.E. said. "Can't you see I've got troubles with the girl? I don't want to be worrying that my daughter's horsing after you all the time. Can you blame me? Put an end to it for me, will you?"

"You poor old feller. You can't have your way this time. As long as your cowboys are ready to take a nose dive and give up the ghost for you, they can almost count on being blessed by you. The minute they show any feelings of their own, you shut down on them. Well, let me tell you something. I didn't bring your girl home to you so I could get your money. I didn't come to fight you for her, either. I came because I'm used to gathering your stock and penning it for you. That's all. You handle her. I ain't taking her to raise."

"That's the way, Bill. You tell him," said Mary.

Bill turned to her and his face was twitching with anger. "And you, stripping and having a runaway in front of a bunch of people. Trying to get your Daddy's cowboys in a fight. That's all you wanted, to have somebody fight over you. Why, I'm surprised your Daddy's so high on you. Why would he even want you around? He don't ever keep that kind of stock."

Bill walked out the door and went back to the El Charro. He found Tom where he had left him. Tony Claire was there in his range clothes, ready to go to work. Tony was happy he had missed Mary's rampage. He said he was also happy he had taken her home at an acceptable hour and was not responsible for her being in trouble, this time. This made Bill figure she probably had gone on other Tucson rampages.

Bill went inside the restaurant to look for the fashion lady. She was doing a dirty black-bottom dance in the center of the dance floor with the heavy, clean-shaven townsman. She had a silly look on her face, and her stockings were sagging around her ankles. Disgusted, Bill turned to leave.

The heavy man yelled, "That's right, go on home, Shane. I'll take care of your woman for you."

Bill knew the voice and the build, the hands, but he was too far away to recognize the man. He stopped to look at him, though. He was not against pausing any moment to do battle with a townsman anywhere in the world.

"Go on, run home," Lindano said. He grinned at Bill and patted the fashion lady with both hands. He picked her up by the waist, held her overhead, and stood her on a table. She sat down and hugged Lindano's sweaty neck and looked straight into Bill's eyes. Bill turned and went out.

Bill did not go back to the patio for more drinks. He left the party and rode back to the herd. He was glad he was going to Mexico. He would never feel at home with the Bradfords again. That Mary was really something and he loved her, but she probably needed a little more age on her. Lordy, she was something, but he had to figure out why she had been so quick to throw in with the Claires again. That was hard for him to take. Did all the Bradfords want him to quit and leave them alone to their money-making?

Bill was beginning to think that R.E. was afraid Bill wanted to own the High Lonesome and Red Rock ranches again. Bill's folks had owned them until their death. They had died in the flu epidemic of 1918 while Bill was in France with the Marines. Claire and his bank had taken over the ranches and then sold them to R.E. Bill still owned thirty sections of the Red Rock Ranch. His folks had put that piece in his name when he went overseas and it was the only land he had not lost when they died. The thirty sections included the land where R.E. had built his home and headquarters. R.E. had been using Bill's part of the ranch just as though he owned it.

Bill had always assumed R.E. did not know Bill owned it. Bill never mentioned it because he did not have the money to stock it himself, and R.E. was keeping up the fences and the watering places. Bill had told Claire he owned the property and shown him the deed when he was trying to borrow money to start his own outfit just before the last cattle drive. He could not imagine R.E. still being ignorant about it. Maybe R.E. meant to stay there until Bill brought it up. Bill had been hoping R.E. would take the initiative toward making it right with him. By waiting for R.E. to make it right, Bill had learned a lot about him, a lot that he did not like.

Bill began to suffer when the effect of the mescal wore off under the mid-afternoon sun. The herd began tiring and was hard to move. Tony and Tom had caught up in time to help move the herd off the bedground that morning, and Bill could see they were slumping in their saddles, too. Tony turned to Bill with a distressed look on his face when Bill rode up to talk to him. Tony was riding a three-year-old colt R.E. had given him.

"Tony, I need you to go to the post office for us," Bill said. "I can see you're just the man to do it, because you don't look so good."

"Listen, I'll do anything to get off this horse and out of the sun."

"The man sells pitchers of cold beer at the post office."

"Just point me to the place."

"All right, ride to the Roblez Ranch and see if our mail caught up. R.E. has been forwarding it there. Drink some beer. Roblez makes good beer. That way your spirit won't depart before you start back."

"Bill, you're saving my life. I'll just change horses and go."

"If you take time to change horses, you'll be too late. The man won't give you the mail after five. He deals with his drunks after five and he won't handle the mail. You have to hook it right now."

"I can't ride this colt that far. I've been riding him all day. He was still juicy at noon, so I didn't catch a fresh horse and now he's wobbling."

"Well, hell," Bill said. "Change horses with me. Ride a good horse for a change."

"Are you sure, Bill? Why not let Tom go? I'm sure he'd appreciate a cold beer."

"No, he deserves to die of his hangover; he's responsible for mine. Here, ride old Lizard."

Bill never loaned his horse to anyone. He wanted to do the boy a favor, but loaning his horse was foolishness. He felt like backing out. *Never loan your horse, your woman, or your pistol* was a cowboy rule. To do it could be a mistake a man might never live down.

Tony hurried to the Roblez ranch. He tied Lizard under a palo verde tree and walked into the open front room of the ranch house. Roblez, a slim and dignified old don, gave him the mail for the crew, poured him a glass of mescal, drew him a pitcher of beer, and went out. Tony waited until he was sure the first swallow of mescal would stay down, then blessed Bill as a saint. Bill had not figured on Tony drinking mescal. Bill had thought a pitcher of beer would be more than enough to cure his pain, but Tony drank all the mescal before he turned to the beer. When he reached for the pitcher, he looked up and saw Lindano coming into the room with a big smile.

"Well, well, it's my old friend and companion of the trail," Lindano said, laughing. "I never thought I'd find you here."

"Is it you, Lindano?" Tony asked. "Good, I've been wanting to talk to you."

"Oh, is that right?" Lindano went to a cabinet, found the mescal bottle, and then drew another pitcher of beer. Roblez came and took his money and went out again.

"What do you want to talk to me about, Tony?" Teasing the boy, Lindano asked, "Will it bother me?"

"I doubt it. I just wanted to tell you that you're the sorriest human I've ever known, that's all. But I'm grateful to you. Because of you I've come to know some good cowboys. You're no hand and you're no man. I found that out. Pour me some more mescal."

"Well, I guess you have good reason to be mad. I know I failed you. Someday maybe you'll understand what I tried to do for you and your father. Let's not argue about it now. I've been wanting to talk to you in private. It's not too late to get even with Shane and the rest of that bunch."

"No. Lindano, I don't want anything to do with you anymore. How I ever came to partner with you I'll never know, except that I wanted to help my dad. I'm sure he didn't know what you were up to either."

"Of course he did. He told me what to do when he hired me."

"No, I don't believe that. You're a spook, Lindano. There's not an ounce of good in you."

Lindano laughed. "I'm no worse than any other man who does business with bankers, Tony. I go where the dollars go."

"You're not normal. I'm on to you. If you're not some kind of spook, then why didn't Bill Shane's spurs split your face in two?"

"Hah. 'Twas the beard and my hate that saved my face.

I'm hard to hurt and impossible to kill, like an old gila monster."

"Well, you're going to apologize to me for the under-handed tricks you pulled on the drive. I'm ashamed you were working for us."

Roblez was listening in an adjoining room. He sold a lot of mescal. He knew its effect on cowboys. He also knew Lindano was coward enough to kill this banker's son over an insult. He picked up his cane and went into the front room.

"Apologize for riding with good men, eating with them, drinking out of the same cup," shouted Tony.

"I apologize," said Lindano, but he winked at Roblez and did not hide it from Tony.

Tony looked pugnaciously at Roblez. Roblez guessed the boy often made trouble for himself, being a rich man's son, well fed and muscular. After riding all day with the sun on his head, the mescal had made him feel too prosperous, too proud of his muscles. He was bound to overmatch himself. He would be lucky if Lindano just coddled him and let him go.

Tony drank awhile longer and then leaned into Lindano's face and said, "If you were a man you'd apologize."

"I already apologized."

"Yes, but I had to make you. You didn't mean it. Why did you walk in here smiling as though you thought I would be glad to see you?"

"Remember, I was working for your father, Tony. I obeyed his orders. You knew what I had to do. Why blame me now?"

"You're an evil spook, that's why. You're a liar, and a thief, and probably a damned murderer, and I was in it with you, that's why."

"You're drunk, but don't call me a murderer. Here, wash out your mouth." Lindano poured Tony's glass full of mescal again. He began watching him closely. "Drink plenty," he said. "It looks like you finally found something you could do."

Tony swallowed all the mescal and beer in front of him and said, "I'll tell you who the best man I know is. Bill Shane. He's the horseman you'd like to be. An evil spook like you can't be a horseman. I've learned one thing, the devil is always afoot, never on horseback, no matter how many horses he would like to ride. And *you* will never make a hand horseback." Tony began to laugh, tickled by this discovery.

"You're drunk," Lindano said. He was not laughing. If Tony could have read his expression, he would have known the man would not take any bullying. The trouble with Tony was that he had been a bully with his fellows in town. He had not learned to read the danger in the expression of a man who was not willing to take his abuse just because he was the banker's son. Lindano had expected to get rich working for Tony's father. Now the father had fired him without a nickel, after Lindano had gone through risk and sacrifice in the banker's scheme to take over the Bradford herd. Claire had put the blame on him for the scheme's failure. Lindano had been fired because he had not been able to keep Shane out of Claire's way.

Lindano decided this was payday. This day he would show Claire why he had hired Mahout Lindano. Lindano was good and mean to unsuspecting horses and gunsels. Sooner or later he always made bigshots like Claire understand why he must be paid.

Tony pushed Lindano. "I'm going to pound on your head, Mahout," he said.

"Don't try, Tony."

"I think I'll just start by beating on your ears."

Lindano grinned and pulled his pistol out of his chaps pocket.

Tony stopped. "That's my pistol, isn't it? I knew you stole it. I knew it, but you wouldn't admit it. You watched me get into trouble over that pistol and you never said a word. Why didn't you give it back to me?"

"I wanted the pistol."

"Give it back." Tony started toward him.

"I'll give you the muzzle blast." Lindano shot Tony through the hand. Tony threw himself at Lindano. Lindano shot him in the leg. Tony fell, but picked himself up.

"Here's your famous pistol for you," Lindano said and he shot Tony through the chest. The boy went down on his back. Lindano sipped mescal as the boy lay dying.

"Now you're a murderer, if you weren't one already," Roblez said. "You'll be hung. I always knew you were a killer."

Lindano emptied his glass and hurried out.

Roblez saw the bright blood from Tony's lungs. The boy was trying to rise and was holding his handkerchief over his wound to keep the blood from spilling. Roblez made him lie down so he could look at the wounds. Roblez's hands were soon drenched in Tony's blood. He looked up and saw that Tony was watching his face.

"It doesn't hurt . . . so don't worry," Tony said. "It's just . . . hard to breathe."

"You're a courageous boy," Roblez said and, he thought, awfully foolish.

"I learned . . . from cowboying . . . that I'm not a coward."

Roblez could not look at the boy's face. Tony tried to joke.

"Courage . . . gave me . . . an awful congestion." Tony smiled to see if Roblez would cheer up. Then he died.

CHAPTER 2

*Some owners figure they must use all of a horse, from his heart
right down to the hair in his tail, if they are to have their money's
worth. When it comes time to turn a horse out because he is worn or
sick, or they see fit to kill him and sell him for his meat, they also
take his hair. They shear off his mane and tail.*

*The hair can be sold to prisons so the convicts can bide their
chains braiding horsehair into chamarra lead ropes, bosal nosebands,
cinches, hatbands, and reins. Shorn of his hair, no matter how he
lights his eye and lifts his tail and plucks his feet from the ground,
a horse can never be complete so long as he is under the stubby,
little, fat, mean, grabbing thumb of a greedy man.*

PASCUAL Matus and the Breach brothers caught up to the
herd the evening Tony Claire was killed. They brought in
strays they had been gathering since the dust storm had
scattered the herd. Bill put down his supper plate and rode
out to help them count the cattle back.

When Bill had come back from his service in France he
had gone to Mexico to help his friend Cabezón Woodell
gather cattle that had been separated from the herd during
the Mexican revolution. Pascual Matus was a Yaqui Indian
chief who was Cabezón's top hand. Bill and Pascual were
compadres. Bill had baptized Pascual's eldest son.

The Mexican government had put a bounty on Pascual's
head after a skirmish in 1924 between the Yaquis and government cavalry at Vicam in Sonora. He had been hiding on
the Apache reservation since then and had joined the High

Lonesome herd when it passed through the reservation on the way to Red Rock. He believed his wife and little daughters had been butchered by General Elias Calles at Vicam.

"I think most of the cows will calve, in spite of their hardship," Pascual said as he looked over the herd. He had not been able to rest for weeks. His Yaqui face was like a block of adobe. He gave Bill no other greeting, just a comment on the condition of the cows.

"Maybe we'll have good luck for a change," Bill said. "I'm glad you're back. A new crop of spotted calves stands up with the cows off the bedground every morning. We have two hundred more cattle than we did when we left the High Lonesome."

Bill saw that Jake Breach was riding Copper, the horse that had fallen on Jonas and killed him. Bill had tried to cut that horse loose. He didn't want anyone riding him from the High Lonesome crew, but this was like Jake Breach to grab a chance to make an extra dollar. Jake probably thought he could pawn Copper off as livestock to someone who did not know any better.

"What do you want with that horse?" Bill asked Jake, when they dismounted at the cook's fire by the wagon.

"Why can't I have him? You didn't want him. What's wrong with him?" Jake said, without turning his face to Bill.

"He's got a notch in his tail. He's a widow maker. You have a wife."

"I tried to tell him," Alex Breach said. "He won't listen. The horse has already bucked him off three times. He hasn't been hurt yet, but Copper'll kill him if he ever gets him in a spot where he can turn a crank with him."

"Why should he go to waste?" said Jake. "Out where I found him he would have starved, been eaten by Yaquis, or died of a broken heart. He won't hurt me. He appreciates me giving him another chance."

"What makes you think the sonofabitch appreciates anything?" Bill asked.

"I just know he does. He carried me here, didn't he? If he carries me a little farther I'll have him where I can sell him and I'll be paid back for being good to him."

"That's just right for him, and you too, I guess," said Bill. He unsaddled his horse. Cap, the cook, handed him another hot plate of beef and beans. Jake sat down next to Bill and kept staring at him. Alex Breach and Pascual had unloaded their pack animals and were eating supper. Bill could tell that Alex was keeping still because he knew his brother was about to start talking business.

"Well, besides making yourself one horse richer, what else is on your mind, Jake?" Bill finally asked.

"I'm going home," said Jake. "I'm soured. Get me off your hands."

"You ain't on my hands, Jake."

"I still have cattle in this herd and I'd like to be paid for them, and I bet you don't have any money."

"None of the stock's been sold, so we don't have any money. We turned some cattle over to the banker, but no money changed hands. We hope we'll be able to sell in May."

"I want my money, and I don't want to sleep with this herd one more night."

"Sleep the hell anyplace you want to. Go sleep near R.E., if you want to sleep near money. He carries the bankroll."

"I made my deal with you. You pay me."

"All right, catch your horses and mules out of the remuda, and pack up, and we'll go find R.E."

"I'm sorry about this, Bill," Alex said. "Jake's ringy."

"That's okay," Bill said. "I have to ride to the Roblez ranch, anyway. I want to see what happened to Tony."

"I'll go, too," said Pascual. "Roblez has mescal."

At nightfall, Pascual, Bill, and the Breach brothers topped a hill above the Roblez ranch and saw a bonfire that was lighting up the swept ground in front of the main house. A crowd of men and horses were around the fire. R.E.

Bradford's roadster was parked there. Badges were shining in the firelight.

The cowboys rode down, and before they were inside the circle of firelight a deputy stood up underfoot and scared their horses. Then a half-dozen deputies came to them and escorted them across the clearing. Bill was identifying himself when R.E. Bradford and Richard Claire came out of the main house.

Claire shook his finger at Bill. "There he is. Hold that man," he said. "Ask him about my son. He's to blame for this."

Bill expected R.E. to say something in his defense, but R.E.'s face was stern and accusing, too. Bill examined his conscience and could not remember one bad thing he'd done that day. He looked around to see if he could find Tony and get some backing from him. He turned to the nearest deputy. "Where's Tony Claire?" he asked, but the deputy ignored him. "Where's Tony?" he asked R.E. Bill's boss turned away.

"Bill Shane?" the sheriff asked.

"Yessir?"

"Get off your horse and come inside. Who are these men with you?"

"They all work with me for R.E. Bradford. We're with his herd."

Bill dismounted and followed the sheriff into the front room. Deputies who had been doing nothing suddenly saw their duty and jumped to Bill's side to make sure he went in after the sheriff. Tony was lying on his back in the middle of the room with the toes of his boots turned in, propped that way by his big spurs. The smell of his blood was strong in the room.

"What happened here?" Bill asked. He wanted to ask, "What happened to my friend?" to show how badly he felt, but he knew Claire would not like him saying Tony was his friend.

"Just explain what my son was doing here, Shane," Claire said. "He's been shot and killed and I know you're responsible."

"Who shot him?" Bill asked.

Roblez came in the room and shook Bill's hand.

"Victor, what happened here?" Bill asked.

"Lindano murdered the boy," Roblez said.

"Why are they blaming me?"

"You had my boy killed to get back at me," Claire said.

"I'd never have anyone killed," Bill said, lamely. He spoke under his breath—no one was listening. Then he realized Claire was trying to make him run, and he got angry.

"I told them Lindano murdered the boy," Roblez said. "He shot him right in front of me. I don't know what else they need to know, or who else they need to blame."

"Lindano kisses *your* fanny, Claire," Bill said. "He does your dirty work, not mine. You paid him to cause dissension on the drive and scatter our cattle. I'm only guilty of loaning Tony my horse so he could come here to get the mail and have a cold beer. By the way, where's my horse?"

"Lindano took him," said Roblez.

Bill looked toward R.E. for support.

R.E. shook his head. "I hate to say it, Bill, but everyone knows you didn't like Tony." He looked away again as though he smelled something bad. "I'd hate to think you were partners with Lindano, but that's how it looks. How come Tony was riding your horse? Didn't he have a horse of his own to ride?"

"I loaned Tony my horse because his colt was tired."

"I have to tell you, it looks funny to me," said R.E. "You never lend your horse to anybody. Not to me, not to Tom, not to anybody, except maybe some little girl you're wooing. Nobody ever rides your horses but you."

"R.E., how can you accuse me of doing the things Lindano does? Anybody who tries to punish me for this murder doesn't want the killer, he just wants me." Bill turned to the sheriff. "I want to know if you're holding me. If you're not, I'm going after the man who shot my friend and stole my horse."

"Aw, I think I'll just keep you," the sheriff said. "I think I'm lucky to have you."

"You partied with Lindano last night," R.E. said. "Mary saw you both at the Pioneer and at the El Charro. Come to think of it, Lindano didn't seem to be hurt much after you put on that big act of hitting him with your spurs. That whole fight could have been put on to make us believe you were enemies. You could have been working together, filching my cattle."

"If you want to know how many cattle were filched out of your herd, ask Pascual Matus over there," Bill said. He just brought in all the dust storm strays. Your herd is now complete. So, I might have been a cowthief to you, but now I'm not."

Roblez stepped forward. "I won't allow these accusations in my house," he said. "I've known Bill all his life. I knew his grandfather, and his father, and all his uncles. He's a good man from good stock. I've known Lindano a long time, too. Men like Lindano never get a chance to run with men like Bill. Mules don't run with racehorses."

Roblez went on by and summoned an Indian boy of about fourteen from another room. The boy was Yaqui. He was barefoot and footsore. Bill knew him. He was Placido, Pascual's son—and he was Bill's godson. Bill thought of him often. He took his responsibility of being the boy's godfather seriously. While he was cowboying for Cabezón Woodell with Pascual in Mexico, he had contributed money so the boy could be sent to study with the Catholic Christian Brothers, a teaching order that had a school in the Yaqui village of Cajeme. He had sent Pascual money to continue the schooling for two years after he left Mexico. He wanted the boy to start his life with a command of the Spanish language. Pascual had been taught his catechism and his Spanish by Franciscan missionaries. Bill had never known a Yaqui or a Mayo who was not a good talker. For centuries the missionaries had been making them good talkers in Spanish while they converted their savage hearts to Catholicism.

Roblez went to the front door and shouted to Pascual. Pascual dragged his spurs into the room, his hat on the back of his head, sweat on his brow. His expression did not change when he saw the boy. He embraced him reservedly, at arm's length. He walked away to a corner with him. The boy began to talk softly and unhurriedly. Pascual listened closely. Then he thanked Roblez and stacked coin on a table to pay for the boy's food and shelter. He led Placido over so he could shake hands with Bill, his *Padrino*.

"How far did the boy come?" Roblez asked. "He said he was looking for you and he said thank-you, and he would not say another word."

"Maybe a hundred leagues," Pascual said. "Thank you for keeping him."

Bill sat down with Pascual at a corner table and Roblez brought them a bottle of mescal. Pascual poured two glasses full and said, "Your business in here kept me from my mescal. What happened, did Tony argue with his papa's *pistolero*? Bad business."

"They're trying to say I'm responsible for Tony's death."

"That boy's father was making him mean. He was always asking to be hurt."

R.E. walked to the table to shake hands with Pascual. Pascual did not stand for him. R.E. stood and waited to be asked to sit. Pascual drank his mescal and did not look at him.

"I hope I'm wrong about you, Bill," said R.E. in Spanish, so Pascual would understand. "I'll not rest until the matter is solved."

"Rest," said Pascual. "You're wrong, so rest about Bill."

"We were talking business, R.E.," Bill said. "You're inter-rupting."

"I won't bother you anymore. I'm glad to see you, Pascual," R.E. said. "Thank you for bringing the strays. The Yaqui boy was at Red Rock looking for you. I brought him here so he would be more comfortable and so he'd be sure and find you. The boy has evidently come a long way. It must be wonderful to inspire such loyalty. No man will ever walk that far for me. Tom Ford, I guess, is the only other man I know who could inspire such loyalty."

Bill wished R.E. would go away. His Spanish was awful.

"I would crawl that far for Bill," said Pascual. "As for the boy, I sired him, so it's easy for me to inspire him. He's my own son Placido. Thank you for bringing him here where he could be fed and rested."

R.E. looked down at Bill. "I have to back Claire and the sheriff, Bill. You'll be charged with conniving with Lindano, and I'm a member of the community that will bring the charges."

Bill looked R.E. in the eye. "Yes, Lindano worked the mischief, and you're down on me for it. Now, you've climbed in bed with Claire because he threatened to slam his bank vault shut and leave you out. You don't mind that he's using his own son's death to drive a wedge between you and your cowboys. He's the cause of his own trouble and you want to believe I am. Why is that? For a money supply. Why are you looking for a reason to run me off? It's money. You have it in your head Mary will marry money for you.

"Listen to me now. Don't be coming around me trying to explain yourself anymore. I can see how pathetic you are without having it all explained to me. You're rid of me. Give me up for dead and rest easy, as Pascual says. Adiós. Go ahead and sell me out, but don't stand there and praise loyalty as if you know what it is. You wouldn't know loyalty if it wiped the sleep out of your eyes every morning.

"I tried to show you respect and stay away from Mary.

Now, I don't respect you anymore and I'm coming to get her. I'll tell you something else, I won't take her far away. That house at Red Rock you thought was just another castle in your empire belongs to me."

"What are you trying to feed everybody, Bill?" R.E.'s face was turning red. "Claire already told me about some claim you think you have. How did you come up with a scheme like that?"

"I'll tell you some more," Bill said. "Keep jumping and biting at your friends every time Claire points his finger at them and pretty soon he'll have you chewing your own flanks—and your friends will run out of loyalty for you."

R.E. nodded and walked away.

"Well, so much for a place to live for the rest of my life," Bill said. "Yesterday morning he promised me a home and a place to work for the rest of my life."

"Listen, Bill. Placido tells me federal soldiers are camped at my mother's ranch at Limón. I have to go. My enemies are calling me home."

"Don't let this trouble keep you here, Pascual. Sooner or later R.E. will wake up and I want to help him. Me and Tom have to stick by him. I haven't done anything wrong, so I'll be all right. You look after your own business."

"Anyway, I can't help you after you take the herd into Mexico. R.E. will ask for protection for his herd from the Mexican army. He hasn't realized how much the generals would give him for me, or he would probably sell me to the government to assure the pasture for his cattle.

"Now, Bill, the best favor you can do yourself is to come with me. Lindano has gone south with your horse. To the north is jail and other trouble for you. Listen, I'll go outside and set Jake Breach to whining. He's in a mood to cause trouble, so I'll tell him the banker has his money. Maybe he'll go for the banker's throat and give you a chance to slip out. We'll bring your horse to the back door."

Pascual got up and went out the front door and the sheriff

walked over to Bill. "I might as well take your pistol, Bill," he said. "Just let me keep it for you so Claire can see it. You don't need to carry it."

Bill handed the man his pistol and thought, Now I've lost my horse, my woman, and my pistol in this lash-up and they're after my good name. I better go with Pascual.

"Please don't drink too much of that mescal," the sheriff was saying. "We'll be heading for town soon and I don't want you to fall off your horse."

"You don't want me to have a drink? You haven't arrested me or charged me, have you?" Bill asked.

"Go ahead and have a drink, if you want to. I'm not charging you with any crime. I think if you and Roblez come to town with us, we can straighten everything out. Just don't drink too much of that hootch, it's against the law."

"I guess I won't. I only drink for fun, anyway."

Claire walked up to the sheriff. "Well, Sheriff, it looks like you're in control, now," he said. "You've solved most of our problems by capturing Shane. There's nothing more I can do here, so I'll go home. I guess you'll take in my son's body, won't you?"

"I'll handle it for you, Mr. Claire," the sheriff said, softly.

Richard Claire turned his back, knelt by his son's body, and looked down into his face. He reached down and gently rested a palm on his brow. Ponderously, wearily, he stood up and started for the door. At that moment, Bill pitied Tony's father. Tony had been foolish and green, but he was a good boy. Bill had lost a good friend and he had walked in on Claire's grief at the wrong time. Claire needed someone to blame, and just the sight of Bill had been enough to throw him into a fit of frenzy.

Jake Breach charged into the room and met Claire with an accounts-receivable look in his eye. Claire had never seen Jake in his life, but he knew the look on his face and that made him hunt an exit. He could see Jake was not bringing him condolences.

"You're Claire?" asked Jake. His eyes had seen dust storms and days without hope, Indian tracks on his cattle's tracks, and green-eyed steers running away. For a month he had been seeing his own ruin instead of stars in the sky when he lay in his blankets at night. Now he thought he could see the man who had his check.

"Aren't you the man who received R.E. Bradford's steers at Red Rock?" Jake asked.

"Yes, but how does that concern you?"

"It concerns me because you are Bradford's banker and partner."

"Well, yes, I'm his banker."

"I know you're the man I want. Pay me for the fifty-seven big steers I brought on this drive. My steers should have gone with Bradford's."

Jake Breach was on the verge of having a final and complete conniption. He was bound to get his money, attack Claire, or throw himself down in a violent fit.

"Don't bother me now," said Claire. "Come to my bank after you've spoken with Mr. Bradford. I'm in no position to argue with you about money. I don't even know you."

"No, but I know you. I'm Jacob Breach, and you're Bradford's money man and I'm at the end of my patience. That's all you need to know."

Placido came in from another room, sat on the floor, and lit a tailor-made cigarette. His hair was wet, and water was running off the points of his sideburns. He released the bright cigarette smoke through his teeth as he examined a sore toe he had just bathed. The examination gave him pain, which he endured silently, almost enjoyably, as he deliberately pressed and kneaded the flesh of his toe. He blew through his teeth for pain, quietly. His concentration was complete. Finally, he found out what he needed to know about his toe, and he tied leather sandals on his feet. He stood, looked at Bill and walked out the way he had come. Bill carried his glass and the bottle of mescal and followed him out. Pascual was mounted and holding Joker. Bill mounted and waited while Placido went for his horse. Alex Breach was also there. When they were all mounted, they rode straight away behind the building so they could keep out of the light of the bonfire. Alex was leading his string of horses and mules. They stopped at the foot of the first hill behind the main building. They did not look back, because the bonfire would blind them to the trail.

"Alex, you're headed the wrong way, aren't you?" Bill asked. "This isn't your way home."

"This is the right way for me," said Alex. "I'll ride behind you so my tracks will be on top of yours. When I head back to the herd, the trackers might follow me. I'm getting away from my brother. He'll never miss me if the banker pays him. I tell you, I've been listening to his bleating so long, I hope he goes back to his wife and leaves me be. From now on, it's a cowboy's life for me."

Pascual put out a hand so Bill would not ride ahead. "I have the tracks of Lizard and Little Pie in this gate," he said.

"Did Placido bring you news of your wife and children, Pascual?" Bill asked.

"Yes."

"Has your wife been found?"

"Yes, Cruz has been found."

"The girls?"

"All alive—and I thought they were dead."

"Ah, you're happy, Pascual."

"What more could I want? I'm on my way home."

Pascual dismounted and opened a wire gate. Bill, Alex, and Placido rode through the gate and stayed off the trail so they would not disturb Lindano's tracks. Pascual tracked Lindano east toward Las Guijas mountains.

"We'll hurry, now and gamble that he stays on this trail," Pascual said. "He'll probably use this trail all the way to the high saddle on Las Guijas. He was bound to hurry for the saddle so he could watch for pursuit."

In the high saddle, Pascual dismounted and lit a match. "Look, here's Lizard," he said, holding the light over Lizard's track. "Here they go, down the *cuesta,* the grade, toward Fronteras."

Placido's horse was stamping nervously beside Joker. Pascual's match went out.

"Is Placido riding Copper?" Bill asked.

"Yes," Alex said.

"Couldn't he have found another horse in the whole state of Arizona?"

"What could he do? Copper was for sale and the boy is sore-footed," Pascual said. "I'll pay Alex for him."

"You won't pay me for him," Alex said. "He doesn't belong to me. I already said you could have any horse in my string. The boy doesn't have to ride Copper."

Bill heard a shout and turned back to the bonfire.

"They're coming now," Pascual said. "Their horses will be tired when they reach this saddle. They smell action, so they'll come on like wild men in the dark, yelling and falling. They'll hurt themselves chasing us. We're quiet and know how to ride trails in the dark, so we'll get away. This is a good place to be an outlaw, this Arizona."

"I'll head back to the herd from here," Alex said. He found Bill's hand and shook it in the dark.

"Stay on this ridge so you'll be easy to follow on your way down," Pascual said. "Your string of animals should make enough noise to draw the sheriff after you."

"I'll wait here awhile until I'm sure they can hear me when I start down," Alex said.

"Thanks, Alex," Bill said.

"Remember, keep your forked end down," Alex said.

"Lindano's headed for Fronteras, all right," Pascual said. "He likes Sin Town. He spends his money there. He'll get drunk and celebrate. The whores and mariachis will occupy him now for a while. We'll catch him on his back with his feet in the air like a cockroach who drank too much Flit."

Pascual led off the saddle. At dawn, he pulled up, and Bill saw Lizard's track again.

"Pascual, how did you know Lindano had not left this trail?" Bill asked.

"Hah, by the sound of my horse's dreadful breathing," said Pascual. "By the stench in my own poor olfactories."

Bill, Pascual, and Placido rode down Sin Street in the zone of tolerance of Fronteras, Sonora, that evening. Three High Lonesome horses were tied in front of the Molino Rojo bar. Bill dismounted and walked in and found Boots Vail, Juan Charro, and Cap Maben—his wrangler, swamper, and cook— drinking at a table. Boots was from an old family of cattle people, and he was young, strong, capable, and hotheaded. Cap had come home old and cranky from the war in France, but he was the best wagon-cook and made the best sourdough biscuits in the state of Arizona. Juan Charro was a derelict who roamed the San Agustín Plains in Western New Mexico. He had the criteria of a coyote and the loyalty of an aged tomcat. He had been a crony of Lindano's for a long time and ran by his side when Lindano was on the plains. They had done such shameful things together they would not admit to others that they knew one another.

"Old Cap didn't have a chance to go to Tucson," Boots said. "So we brought him here and stayed to watch over him while he blows out. We want to be sure he makes it back to the herd in time to cook breakfast."

"That's fine," Bill said.

"Come to think of it, us wranglers didn't get to Tucson like everybody else." Boots was nervous. He was probably thinking he had been caught afoot and doing wrong too far away from his work with the herd.

"It's all right," Bill said. "I'm glad to see you."

"It's my fault we're here," Cap said. "I'll take the blame for us leaving the herd. My soogans need airing just like everybody else's. I was getting so sour I couldn't catch my teams in the morning."

"Cap, you're not in trouble. I need you here." Bill could see they had been taking their drinks slowly, enjoying their time away from the herd without blowing the lid off the town. "Do me a favor and don't leave until I get back here to have a drink with you."

"Sure, Boss. We'll be here," Boots said. It never occurred to Bill that he had no right to ask the cowboys to back him in his trouble with Lindano. They were his partners.

Bill went back outside and Pascual pointed down the street with his chin. Little Pie, Lindano's horse, and Lizard were tied under a mesquite in an alley between the Molino Rojo and The Paris Nights bar. Placido had tied Copper by Lizard and was squatting under the tree.

The Paris Nights was Zuni Jaquez's bar. Zuni was Bill's friend when Bill was drinking. Zuni was a gentleman, but he lived for his drunkenness. He was a successful and accomplished drunkard, with gamey adventures to his credit. He drank more of his own spirits than his customers did. He always drank with his customers, at any hour. Anyone who drank was his friend. He kept a fifty-five-gallon barrel of mescal in a patio behind his bar so he would never run dry.

Lindano's voice was loud in the cantina. He sounded like a feeding glutton, now that he felt at home. Zuni appeared in the door and recognized Pascual and Bill. Bill saw Lindano through the open door. A woman was dancing on the bar and Lindano was using his big sheath knife as a baton, directing her feet. Three worn instrumentalists were in a corner playing music for him. Bill could see they had been playing long past the limits of their stamina, but Lindano was not letting them go home. Lindano's back was to Bill, but Bill could see the edges of his grin as his head swayed from side to side with the music.

Pascual motioned for Zuni to keep silent. Zuni turned back into the bar and closed the door. Bill rode Joker down the side of the building and tied him in the back. He walked to a window and looked in. Zuni was helping a woman down off the bar. The woman was the fashion lady.

The fashion lady was bare-legged and barefoot. Her hair was in her eyes. Her dress was torn, soiled, and twisted on her body as though someone else had dressed her and she did not care enough to straighten it. She was drunk, and her face was swollen and bruised. A lot of moisture had been summoned into her face by weeping.

"Put the old doll back up there," growled Lindano. "I'm not through with her. You can have her when I leave."

Zuni was not a meticulous man. He wore no diamonds. He was pale and bald-headed, small, uncared for, and unshaven. He was too small to gather much dirt, and so he was not much soiled. His worst vice, almost his only vice, was his drunkenness. He drank pure spirits of mescal, and so his drunkenness did not even include base gluttony. His habitual drunkenness had never done away with his careful upbringing, his knowledge of the meanness of wrongdoing, and the worth of valorous behavior.

"Man," said Zuni, smiling at Lindano. "The lady can't dance on my bar. She's smudging the shine and showing indecent portions of her legs to my patrons."

"You're too proud of your dump," Lindano said. "You're just too *presumido*—you presume too much for a friendly little drunk—if you think you can tell me how to use my women."

"I presume nothing," Zuni said. "The vice of drink afflicts me and I can't have much pride. My vices, however, do not include allowing the torture of my patrons."

Zuni turned his back on Lindano and walked out the back door. Bill found Pascual and sat in the shadows of the night and waited.

"Isn't it time I went in and shot him, Pascual?" Bill asked. "Why am I waiting? He's come far enough."

"A bad place for it," said Pascual. "Too early. He's not so easy to shoot and you might kill a musician. Do you know how much trouble you can have if you shoot a musician in Mexico during the performance of his art?'' Pascual laughed. "Let's wait until he gets drunk, or so entertained by his tormenting drunks and whores that he doesn't see us coming. Let's wait at least until I find you a pistol. What do you think?''

"That poor woman isn't a whore,'' Bill said. "She's my friend.'' He was squatting on his heels with his back to the wall.

"I'll go find us some food,'' Pascual said. "Meat, tortilla, and drink will take murder off your mind. Whatever you do, don't go in there. The man's blood is up with his bullying and you're no match for him. If he gets by you, we might loose him. Wait until I come back.''

Bill squatted against the wall and listened to Sin Town. He became aware of a presence of evil he had never noticed there before. The sounds from the cantinas and bordellos fell silent every so often, as though the town wanted to listen a moment while it chewed. When the sounds resumed, they were like growls of pleasure from a demon who was there to feast and was being brought too little fare. It wanted more. Murder would be good.

Men arrived and piled out of roadsters and disappeared in the maw of the demon. Men were having fun throwing themselves in as a staple for the feast. Every now and then the demon coughed them back into the street so they could laugh and take their breath and enjoy their danger before they cast themselves back in again. The demon gulped them all as they came in range.

A group of small boys played into the street. These boys lived by running errands for the whores while they languished and rekindled themselves during the day, before the demon awoke to its full appetite at dark. Now, the boys were at their playtime and careful to stay out of reach of the maw while the demon was feeding. They were playing mustang, a game boys in southern Arizona and northern Sonora played to enjoy freedom. Every boy was a wild mustang at the beginning of the run except the boy carrying a lariat, who was "it." The boy who was "it" was the cowboy and he had to rope and capture a mustang and make him "it."

The boys ran and played with bravery, risk, and headlong fun up and down the street. Bill was enjoying the game until a sharp scream from inside the Paris Nights stopped the boys in flight, stopped even the demon's growl. Bill hurried to the saloon and stepped inside the door. Lindano had taken hold of the fashion lady's foretop and was sawing it off with his sheath knife. He jerked away the last strands of hair and turned his back and left her crying on the floor with her hands on her head. He had cut off all the hair on the top of her head at the scalp. He laughed and pointed at her with the hand that held the hair.

"Ah, finally, I can see the little face. I haven't been able to see it lately with the hair in it. Why, she's no doll. Her magic is gone now that she's plucked."

The fashion lady jumped to her feet and shrieked again and Lindano flourished his knife at her throat. "I'll cut out your gizzards if you don't shut up," he said. "Close your mouth, you're ugly."

As he turned to the musicians to order them to play, Lindano saw Bill. "My partner," he shouted. "I see you, partner of the trail. Come on and have a drink."

Bill went to the fashion lady and helped her sit down in a corner with her back to the wall. Zuni stepped between Bill and Lindano.

"Come on, friend Shane," Lindano said, looking over Zuni's head. "Have a drink. Have a woman. Take that one. You remember her, don't you? She was almost yours. I'm just about to turn her out. I trimmed her mane. She's all used up for a while. See? I've pulled off her shoes and trimmed her mane. I won't need her for a while. I'll make a bracelet of her foretop and give it to you for a keepsake. See, I left some mane on the sides so the flies won't bother

her ears. She's been ridden so hard she hasn't the strength to fight the flies. You take her, Shane. Fatten her. Shoe her. Let her grow a new foretop. Make her healthy for me again."

Lindano moved toward Bill. "Here, Salted Shane. Dance with the woman. She's footsore from running with me, but she ought to be just right for you. You ought to be footsore, too, since I took your horse. I took your horse and your woman, Shane. Are you too footsore to move, too sad to dance? Dance with her. Humor me."

"Bill is not a dancer," Zuni said.

"Never mind, Zuni," Bill said in Spanish. "I can say no to the son of a bitch."

"Hah, what are you calling me, exactly? Son of a dog? Listen, here in Mexico you're nothing but a common gringo, and I'm not your dog to whip."

"Listen, Lindano. You're going back to Tucson with me to hang for killing Tony Claire," Bill said in English.

"Oh, no. Today, I'm drinking. I'm a bigshot today, like *you*."

Lindano shoved a table against Bill, pinning him against the wall. Lindano was so strong and full of meanness that he surprised Bill. Bill had thought he would be a whole lot more respectful and timid with the man who had hit him in the mouth with a pair of spurs. Lindano held Bill against the wall with the table, drew his pistol, and fired into the wall by Bill's ear. The music stopped. The musicians ran for the doors. Lindano waved his pistol and shouted at them. His shout rerouted them so they scattered for the windows instead of the doors. They left the place with banging strings and rattling horns. Lindano threw back his head and laughed. Bill lunged for the pistol. Lindano moved his pistol arm enough to make Bill lose his balance and then dropped the pistol barrel on Bill's ear. He poked the pistol into Bill's chest and shoved him back against the wall. He took the fashion lady by the wrist and whipped her around so she hit the wall beside Bill. Bill's ear was bleeding. He pressed his handkerchief against it.

"You're hurt," the fashion lady said to Bill. She took the handkerchief from Bill and pressed it to his ear again.

"Get away from him," ordered Lindano, and he jerked the table aside.

"Let him alone, now, he's bleeding," said the fashion lady.

"He doesn't need his blood. He's dead."

Lindano aimed for Bill's kneecap and shot him through the flesh above the knee. Bill fell on his face in the corner. The fashion lady bent over him and when Lindano came closer to shoot Bill again she straightened and hit him on the cheek with a tiny fist. Lindano stumbled as though the blow had stunned him.

"Get away, or I'll hit you again," said the fashion lady, fiercely.

Lindano smiled and aimed his weapon at the girl's stomach. Zuni rushed him from the side, shoved the pistol away, and pushed the fashion lady so she fell on top of Bill. Zuni stepped back and cocked his own fist so he could hit Lindano. He whimpered because he was doing something he did not want to be doing. Lindano shot him through the stomach. Zuni staggered into Bill's corner. Lindano shot him again and stacked him on top of Bill and the fashion lady. Then he emptied the pistol on the heap of people in the corner.

A bullet skipped across Zuni, grazed off the fashion lady, and went into the back of Bill's shoulder, causing him to convulse under the dead weight of Zuni and the fashion lady. Another slammed the wall by his head and covered him with a batter of blood and calcimine. The last bullet went through the cheeks of the fashion lady's fanny and flew on, ending Zuni's life at the moment he had given himself a chance for salvation, the moment he offered his life for his friends. Lindano had let his bullets go in random flight to see what evil or good they might do. A kind of good-humored demon must have been prowling in him, a demon who was content to leave to chance and physics the effect the unaimed bullets might have. That demon gave up on taking Zuni's drunkard's soul at the moment Zuni offered his body to protect his friends. The same demon let Bill live so he could seek revenge, and allowed the fashion lady to live so she could go home and be a disgrace to her circle of nice people.

Pascual heard the shooting and hurried to Zuni's bar, but he did not see Lindano. The people in the bar said Lindano had walked away laughing.

Pascual and the High Lonesome cowboys sent for a doctor and moved Bill and Zuni and the fashion lady to the nicest room on the street, the madam's room in the Molino Rojo. They deposited Bill and the fashion lady side by side on the bed and left Zuni on the floor. Three nuns came in with the doctor and helped the whores strip the victims so the doctor could work.

Bill watched Zuni when the girls rolled him over. Zuni was not watching anything. "Is Zuni dead?" Bill asked a whore named Lydia.

"Yes, your friend is dead," said Lydia.

"Close his eyes, will you please?"

"Whoocha, he wants to look at me," Lydia said. She pushed gingerly down on his eyelids with the tip of one finger. She stopped, then tried again.

Bill relaxed and closed his own eyes. He had been holding his breath. He knew he was to blame for Zuni and the fashion lady. He turned to her. She was on her side watching him while the doctor and the nuns made a crowd over her tattered fanny, repairing it.

"I'm glad you're okay," she said. "I'm sorry I caused this trouble. You should not have come after me. No one else cared, why did you?"

"No," Bill said. "I should have let you alone at the Pioneer before anything happened." He did not have it in his heart to tell her he had not thought of her since he had last seen her at the El Charro, that he had no idea she was here.

"Don't forget, you owe me a horse," she said.

"I haven't forgotten," Bill lied. He thought, what horse could I give her? Not Steeldust, by God. Not Lizard, either. I'm not so guilty of anything I have to give the old tart a good horse.

The doctor told Boots to come forward, and then all available whores, nuns, cowboys, and cooks took hold of Bill while the doctor dug the bullet out of his shoulder. He held up the bullet, and Bill fainted away into a cool, dark place while the whores cleaned him up.

That evening, Pascual was sitting with Boots, Cap, and Juan Charro in the Molino Rojo when Lindano walked up and pounded his bludgeon quirt on their table.

"*¿Que clase de demonio es este?* What class of demon is this?" asked Pascual, taken completely by surprise.

Boots looked down at Lindano's feet, wondering how so large an enemy could have arrived so silently at their throats. Lindano was wearing Chihuahua spurs that were heavy with silver and gold inlay. Their big rowels should have had a ring that could be heard down the street when they were dragged over a walk or a floor, yet they had made no sound. Lindano had wired the rowels so they could not roll and glance along a horse's hide. Tied down, they could only gouge. Tied down, they could not ring and warn a horse he better move because they were on the way. They sneaked up on a horse and hooked into him and made Lindano feel good. By making them still, stopping their rolling and their ringing, Lindano had taken away their soul. He tasted blood each time he spurred a horse.

"Hate me. Hate me," Lindano growled, laughing. "It gives me pleasure." He stared down at Juan Charro who was the only one at Pascual's table not looking him in the eye. Juan Charro was looking at the bubbles in his beer and pulling the hair by his ear. He sighed and brushed his nose. He tasted his beer. "You don't hate me, do you, Juan Charro?" Lindano asked. "You and I were friends, but you betrayed me. I was nice to you, but you turned away from me and joined these men who hate me."

"You are only an instant from death, Lindano," Pascual said. "Make an act of contrition."

"Why do you want to kill me?" cried Lindano. "I've come to see if I could talk to you, spend some time and explain myself to you, my comrades of the trail. Too bad about Tony, but he was a hothead. You all knew that. I shot him in self-defense. Too bad about Bill Shane, too. He was jealous of me, and I couldn't calm him any other way except by killing him.

"What else could I do? I'm a man. I didn't shoot them until they threatened me."

"Shut up, horse thief, *robabestias*," said Pascual. "Defend your skin against the wrath of God, if you can."

"Listen, I might lose my skin to the wrath of God, but never to a drunk in a bordello. You'll skin my chile for me, *that* is what you can skin, if you're good to me and I let you."

Lindano pulled his pistol and backed toward a side door. Pascual picked himself out of his chair, puffed on his cigarette, and followed him. Boots walked with Pascual, eager to back him.

"Wait, young man," said Pascual. "Let's see if this great horseman can mount his horse and fly away. Horseback, he's like a wingless fly the toad turned loose."

Lindano hurried to the tree where Lizard and Little Pie were tied. Placido was still holding Copper there. Lizard saw Lindano and raised his head. The whites of his eyes showed in the lantern light of the Molino Rojo. He tightened his butt and began to tremble. Copper was standing against Lizard's left side, leaving no room for Lindano to take his stirrup and mount. Copper measured Lindano's approach with a mean eye. Lindano tried to wedge his way between the two horses' hips, but Copper backed his ears and sidled against Lizard and danced on his hind legs and switched his tail at Lindano. Lindano persisted, and Copper crowded against Lizard and kicked at Lindano. Lindano swore and walked around to the tree where Lizard's rein was tied. While he reached to untie it with one hand, he raised his pistol to strike Copper and get even with the other. Copper jerked away from Placido. Lizard snorted and jerked back and caught Lindano's ring finger inside a loop in the rein and then shook his head with all his weight until the rein broke.

Lindano screamed and all three horses broke away together and ran down the street. Lindano dropped his pistol and reached into the tree to free his finger, screaming like a siren. Pascual picked up the pistol and Boots cut Lindano loose.

Inside the Molino Rojo, Pascual laid Lindano on his face over a table and tied his hands behind him. The finger that had been caught in the rein was hanging by a shred of tendon. Pascual trimmed it off with Lindano's sheath knife. Lindano bellowed as though the owls had him until Pascual pursuaded an ill-humored whore to come and give him mescal and dress the stump. Finally, he quieted.

"Now, let's enjoy ourselves awhile," Pascual said. "Let's see if Lindano's finger grows back and heals as quickly as they say his lip healed after Bill split it with his spurs." Pascual poured all their glasses full and toasted Lindano. "Mahout, may you feel healthy until you hit your head on the hangman's knot, that the finger Lizard chopped off hurts like fire until the very last instant of your life."

Pascual and the High Lonesome cowboys celebrated until midnight when Pascual realized he was too drunk to perform the formal business of giving Lindano to the authorities. He stood up.

"We've done everything we came here to do, except put this man in his cage. I'll go rest now. Somebody should go tell the gringos we have their murderer, though. Wake me when they come for him. I'm drunk."

Pascual went away to the madam's room to sleep on the floor. Boots crossed the border to look for a telephone and an officer of the law. Cap passed out in his chair with his head on the table while a whore was pulling on his arm for attention.

Juan Charro soon tired of guarding Lindano. Dawn was about to catch him sleepless and full of beer and desolately sober. He was dreading the ride back to the herd and the day's work. Lindano had been sleeping, so Juan Charro fell asleep with his chin on the table, his face only inches from Lindano's. When he awoke he looked straight into Lindano's gaze.

"Don't believe them. You know I'm a fair man," Lindano said softly.

"Pascualito does not say so," Juan Charro said. He'll see you hung. I wouldn't question him about that."

"Pascual is a drunk and he makes mistakes."

"I have never known Pascualito to make a mistake."

"Well, he's made one this time. I have a clear conscience. Claire paid me nothing. He beat me out of my wages. I should have been paid extra for the kind of work I did. The priests and nuns who preach the catechism will tell you that the one sin that cries to heaven for vengeance is the sin of defrauding a man of his wages."

"I don't remember my catechism and I never heard that part."

"I remember my catechism and I tell you that part is true. These gringos defrauded me."

"Yes, I can see it would discredit a man to shoot the boss's son to death."

"I shot a big and powerful young man who was attacking me."

"That's true, I guess."

"I knew you would understand, Juan. I knew I could

appeal to you. It's a wonder the gringos haven't turned on you too. They never seemed to like you. They haven't paid you, either, have they?''

"True, and also they didn't buy my cows. They bought everyone else's, but not mine."

"You're lucky you didn't bring them your cows. The gringos didn't pay anyone for their cows. You see now how they've treated us?"

"What you say seems to be true."

"Now I'm to be hanged for standing up for my rights, for asking for my wages, and for defending myself. How do you think I feel, Juan? Do you remember the afternoon we spent in the meadow in the mountains of Capitán last year? Only a year ago it was. Remember when we robbed the bee tree? How sweet and clear that honey was, remember? The way I got it out, neither of us got stung, remember? You loved that honey in the fall.''

"I remember. I'd do anything to be there now. Do you suppose we'd find honey in that tree again?"

"Of course, that country is full of honey. If you want to go back we can go together. Untie me before somebody comes. If you're not here when they come back they won't blame you. They'll blame the cook, or the whores. I'll meet you on the other side of the border at noon."

Juan Charro untied Lindano. When Boots returned at eight o'clock in the morning with an old, sleepy-headed constable and a Mexican cop, Lindano was gone. Juan Charro was never seen again. He did not call at Red Rock for his wages, and he never returned to his camp on the San Agustín Plains.

CHAPTER 3

*Every horse has at least one talent useful to man. He learns to
do wrong only through man. He learns to do well if his trainer has
good sense. A horseman has the responsibility to find and develop
a horse's talent.*

*Every horse alive can do at least one chore helpful to man. He
may have no quickness for cutting, but great stamina as a circle
horse. He may not be smooth-gaited enough to carry a man on a
forty-mile circle without killing him, but have explosive speed for
catching cattle in rough country.*

*One man might not have work for a certain horse. Another might
be able to depend on the same horse for his livelihood. The value of
a horse depends on the need he satisfies in a man, a woman, or a
child. One man might not give a quarter for a horse that another
man would be happy to buy for five hundred dollars. It might be
true that every man has a horse that would be good for him, waiting
for him somewhere.*

OUTSIDE the Molino Rojo, Lindano had been careful he
did not hurry up behind the horses in the dark, a lesson he
should have learned before it cost him a finger. Lizard had
been taken away to rest and feed, but Little Pie and Copper
had been caught and returned to the same tree. Lindano
mounted Little Pie and led Copper away. He rode to his
uncle's house on the edge of town and hid the horses in his
aunt's adobe wash shed.

Lindano's old uncle came to the door of the shed while
he was unsaddling Little Pie. Lindano's abuse of his aunt
and uncle through his teen years had intimidated them so

they never refused him whenever he showed up. The uncle saw Lindano's hand was tied in a bloody rag and stepped forward to help him. He carried grass and mesquite beans to the horses and spoke to them.

Lindano's aunt dressed the stub of his finger at her kitchen table. He sweated from the pain and bragged about his horses. He told his aunt and uncle he was taking the two sorrels to the Yaqui River to sell to a colonel of the Mexican cavalry. He told of another sorrel horse, called Steeldust, that was winning fame under his training. His uncle and aunt would soon hear of this horse because he was bringing him to Mexico. This horse would make him rich and famous. He had roped the big bull and turned back a thousand cattle on Steeldust. He told his aunt and uncle of the herds of cattle he was bringing down the trail for the gringo millionaire, R.E. Bradford, and the American bankers. He asked his aunt and uncle if they needed money. If they did, he would write them a check, or if they could wait for a few days he would have his American bank wire them cash. From now on, he would be supplying them money. He laid a fifty-dollar gold piece on the table for them. The fifty dollars was for keeping his esteemed horse, Little Pie, and for the other horse, Copper, and for provision. He wanted to be sure his aunt and uncle were well provisioned.

Lindano told his aunt and uncle he had just killed a man, maybe two men and a woman, in the Paris Nights bar. They would soon hear about it. He was innocent of blame. Three people had attacked him and he had fought alone. He did not want them to tell anyone he was visiting them, though. He would be cleared as soon as he could rejoin his associates in the government.

The aunt and uncle watched every word as it came out of Lindano's mouth and gave mumbled lip service to it. They already knew of the fight in the Paris Nights. They knew Lindano was probably guilty, but the gold piece made them forgive him. They were sure their ship had finally come in.

This just proved no one could ever tell how God was going to send His help.

The uncle began feeling as expansive as Lindano. He told Lindano the fifty-dollar gold piece would do him and he did not think he needed to be wired money or written a check. He hitched his milk cow to his cart the next morning and drove her to a neighbor's field. He filled the cart with alfalfa he cut with his sickle. He paid his neighbor with *centavos* he and his wife had been saving, a few coins with which he and his wife had become well acquainted. They had counted and recounted the coins so many times they knew them as well as they knew each other's faces. The coins were as much a part of them as each other's faces. He prodded the cow home and carried the alfalfa to the horses. He carried water to them and made a show of tasting it so Lindano could be sure it was potable.

Lindano's aunt and uncle made their living as servants in the whorehouses. They cleaned the rooms and ran errands. The aunt made tortillas and prepared snacks and lunches for the whores. She sold the whores eggs and milk and prepared the nogs for their morning hangovers. The uncle carried cold beers to the whores' clients so they could refresh themselves while they were dressing.

Lindano rested all day. At nightfall he saddled Little Pie, skirted the town, crossed the border, and headed north.

Mary was at Red Rock. She had quit school the morning after her rampage. She had been sleeping as though stricken with a brain fever.

She felt Bill had backed down from her father and quit her just when she believed he loved her. Her father had made up his mind he needed a banker and expected Mary to help woo him. She had been expected to marry Tony and now was expected to make a show of mourning him. Her father and mother were telling people she was ill because Tony had been killed. She was sad about Tony, but losing

Bill had made her ill. She had been holed up, swelled up, and sulled up like a mad brahma cow ever since her rampage.

Mary was looking out her window at the back of Steeldust's stall, realizing she was neglecting him. The Red Rock cowboys had been feeding him. She had been too worthless to go and see how he was doing. She would rather lie moribund in her bed. She saw a flash of sorrel hide pass between the barn and Steeldust's stall, and she wondered if someone was taking him out.

"Mary? Mary?" Her mother was speaking sweetly to her and tapping on her door. Mary had locked her out.

Mary decided her troubles were all a matter of stance. Her former stance had been that of a comfortable coed in a society of people engrossed in getting everything it wanted. Bill's stance had been that of a man who did not give a particular damn about society or having a damn thing except his horse. She and Bill might have loved the way they lived, but they both would regret the love they let die because of their stances.

They were open to the lies people could tell them that would keep them in their places. R.E. had told her Bill was running with Lindano and that he had sent Tony into an ambush to be killed. While Bill was running from the sheriff, he had been shot in a whorehouse brawl and was on a drunken binge while he recovered, a strange new stance. Mary was supposed to believe that and the burden of it had kept her in bed waiting for rescue, relief, or death—her new stance.

She did not like R.E.'s new stance, either. All of a sudden he was chasing the almighty dollar too almighty much and acting proud of it.

"Mary, you'll have to come out of there, now," said her mother. "I'm cooking bacon and eggs for you."

Mary pushed back her covers and stood up. She opened the window and the fall day gave her fresh air. Her cottonwoods by the window waved and turned the silver sides of their leaves to her in a little breeze. She dressed in a shirt and sweater, Levis and boots. She hurried because she wanted to see who was with Steeldust. Maybe Bill was down there.

She hurried out the front door with her mother calling after her. She ran with her swollen eyes opening to the day, ashamed she had buried herself so long. If Bill was here she was about to scare him to death. She had been lying on her face for a week. She rounded the corner of the stall and saw no one with Steeldust. He was still in his stall. She walked into the barn and Little Pie was feeding on the haystack. He raised his head and looked at her guiltily. She wondered how Little Pie could be at Red Rock. Everyone in the country was chasing Lindano. He was supposed to be a hundred miles south, running for his life. Mary turned at a sound in the grain barrel. Lindano was filling a morral with grain. He straightened and grinned at Mary. No one in that country would have begrudged the grain to anyone but him, and he was grinning because he knew it.

"Hello, I thought you'd been fired," said Mary.

"Ah, you know me?" asked Lindano. "What's my first name?"

"Who cares? Your last name is sheep dip."

"Mahout is my first name. Call me Mahout."

"What kind of a name is that? Who could remember that name?"

"Ah, more people every day, Miss Mary. My name is something important."

"You have an awful gall, considering you're a murderer and I just caught you in my daddy's grain barrel. Does Mahout mean murderer and sneak thief, or is a Mahout just another kind of rat? You'd better leave before our cowboys catch you. They won't call the sheriff to come get you. They'll drag you through the cholla until you're nothing but a jerky."

"No cowboys here this morning, missy. They've all gone to the herd to bring back more cattle your banker bought."

"Lucky for you. They'd drag your bones to the sheriff for killing Tony Claire."

"That was self-defense. Self-defense. I had the right to kill him."

"They say you shot Bill Shane."

"Self-defense."

"You're telling me you really did shoot Bill? Was he asleep? Was he drunk, or did you shoot him in the back?"

"He was trying to take my woman. What could I do? He wanted my woman. I had to protect her."

"Where is he?"

"In the place where I shot him, unless they buried him. If he's not dead he's still with the whores having a good time."

"Liar."

Lindano laughed. "Yes, I've been lying, Missy. Bill and I have always been friends. We wanted people to think we were enemies. He sent me to bring you to him. He wants to see you before he leaves the country. Me, Bill, and Pascual are headed south together. Bill's never coming back."

"Hah, go on and lie. Bill would never send you to get me. Bill's friends are men like Tom Ford and Boots Vail, Cap Maben and my Daddy. He's no friend of yours."

"Don't you believe he loves Pascual Matus, either? He does. Pascual is also my friend."

"Maybe that's true, but I never understood how anybody with any good in him could be a friend of Pascual's."

"Well, Pascual is yonder in the brush waiting to take you to Bill."

"Why isn't he here instead of you?"

"Ah, I know where the grain barrel is. I worked here. I knew where to find the Steeldust horse. Pascual did not. He told me, if you saw me near the horse, you'd come running. He was right. Now, you can come with me and no one will know. Pascual's wise. I'll saddle Steeldust for you."

"Why didn't Bill come? He could hide in the brush the same as anybody else."

"Unfortunately he's been hurt. Not seriously, though."

"Bring Pascual here, then."

"No, I'm here. Pascual isn't wanted by the sheriff. He can head off anybody who approaches the ranch by stopping them and talking to them."

"I'll tell you, Lindano, I think a lot of Bill Shane, but I don't think enough of him, or anybody else, to ride off with you and Pascual Matus. If I wanted to ride with Pascual, which I don't because he's just another cutthroat, I wouldn't go with you."

"Nevertheless, I have to follow my orders. You're riding with me today." Lindano led Steeldust from his stall and saddled him with Mary's saddle. "You see, Miss Mary, I know you love your mother and wouldn't want me to rape and strangle her."

Mary marched toward the door. Lindano jerked out his sheath-knife and held it under Steeldust's belly.

Mary stopped. "What are you doing?"

"Nothing that would bother you, I suppose, Miss Mary," said Lindano. "Only, if you leave, I'll open the horse's belly and drop his guts on his feet. It'll be your fault. Once I taste blood and see you crying, I'll go to the house and surprise your mother. In the last few days that I've been watching her, I've grown to love the way she sings when she does her housework. I love your mother's voice. I'll have her scream and cry for me. Then it'll be your turn to cry, and so on. You'll be surprised at the things you can do with your intestines piled on your feet."

"Dirty murderer."

"Yes, also horse thief, horse killer, horse eater. I'm not just a murderer. Call me anything you like and you'll probably be right. I'll do anything to get what I want and right now I want you and this horse. I've not wanted anything else since I saw you riding him in the cottonwoods on the High

Lonesome. Now, get on him, or I'll spill his guts. If you want to ride him and not some other horse, get on him right now."

"I know you always wanted him. You won't kill him."

"I'd as soon have him dead as alive, if you don't get to moving. He's mine, as you are mine, dead or alive. See how big and easy he is? See how he stands and turns his side to us, trusting us both and waiting for your whim to decide whether or not I'll split him open?"

"Where's Bill?"

"Halfway between here and where we're going."

"The whole world will come after you."

"Mount the horse, or I'll go say goodbye to your mama for you. You think she'd like that?"

Mary turned Steeldust around and mounted. Lindano mounted Little Pie, took Steeldust's lead rope, and led Mary away. Tears started in Mary's eyes. Lindano stopped, peered into her face, and laughed.

"Don't cry, Missy. You were born to ride this horse with me. You've never been worth more than you are right now. You're Mary, clean and bright, born for me, Mahout Lindano. Think of it. Be happy you're finally worth something."

Mary swung a fist at Lindano's face. She had never hit anyone before. Lindano caught one hand and looped his piggin' string on her wrist, passed the string through the gullet of her saddle, and then tied her hands together. He turned away and led Steeldust at a high lope toward the south.

Lindano had never been able to tie cattle or horses so handily. He was always afraid of being kicked or bitten. But he was good at tying women, even with a sore hand, if they were not too big. He had given himself a lot of practice, and a girl Mary's size could not hurt him. He even liked girls to fight back. He figured he must be the best kidnapper in the western world. Every man should do what he does best, if he is to be happy.

Even though he was heavily muscled, Steeldust was smooth-gaited. He fell into a soft canter. He had learned to save himself and move smoothly since the first days his dam had made him run forty miles with her to and from water. He had learned to carry weight on long circles with Bill Shane. He cradled Mary and soothed her and stayed under her. Mary was a fine horsewoman, and she dozed and rested often without losing her balance.

Lindano was too heavy for his horse, and he set a pace that was killing Little Pie. Little Pie was bighearted, but small and rough-gaited. He could not adapt to catching and inter-cepting Lindano's bulk when it was headed for the ground. Lindano used his butt as his bearing surface, and since it was round like his head, he was always off balance. Like most men who spend their lives riding on their butts with their feet hanging down, he had a high tolerance for pain in his tail. His horse launched him into free space with each jump and provided a moving, bony, gritty platform for his landing. The impact Lindano made each time he came down shook sweat off the horse and chipped Lindano's gritted teeth.

If Lindano had known the traditions of horsemanship, he might never have tried to become a horseman. He would have been handier and happier as a murderer and kidnap-per, afoot in the secret alleys of a city. The Arabs who wooed, loved, and warred on horseback for centuries would have told him his judgment and ability did not serve him well as a horseback abductor of ladies. The first thing any good horseman did when he decided to ride away with a lass was choose the right horses. If he had only one smooth-gaited horse available for an abduction, he would do best to ride the smooth-gaited horse and let the lady ride the rough-gaited horse, so she would be sure to swoon into his arms when he helped her down at his tent.

Thus, Lindano's hurry and his own saddle horse were on Mary's side against him. Knowing he had to stay away from decent people kept him off balance, too. He suffered from a self-conscious fear that required him to be completely in secret with a woman in order to do the things he wished to do to her. That was why the fashion lady was still alive. All he had ever done to her was fill her with whiskey, blacken her eyes, and make her dance for the crowd so he could show off. The fashion lady had gone with him more or less voluntarily, and because of that, he had no desire for her.

Now that he had Mary and the law was after him, he would not be able to satisfy himself until he could take her to the edge of the world and have a few days' rest. He would not have the courage to take hold of her and count a score for his venture any other way. He had a place on the edge of the world, but it was still far away. Soon he would be in Mexico and out of jurisdiction of the law for a while, and all he had to do was hurry and get Mary out of sight to have what he wanted.

Lindano reached Fronteras in the early morning. He stopped with the lights of the town in sight. He felt at home. He liked the music of the saloons. He liked to sleep there and wake up to the smells of mesquite smoke and toilet water. Mary was sleepy, but because of Steeldust's smoothness and power, she was not aching. Lindano was so tired he was shaking. He had been standing in his stirrups a lot to ease the sores on his tailbone.

"We're stopping so you can rest," Lindano said. "Remember this. These people are used to seeing men ride in with stolen girls. They're used to hearing girls cry for their mamas. If you run away, I'll have plenty of help to bring you back."

Lindano rode on to his uncle's house, unsaddled the horses, hid them in the wash shed, and led Mary into his aunt's kitchen. The uncle went away to cut alfalfa. Lindano introduced Mary to his aunt as his new wife. The old lady did not raise her eyes to look at Mary. She fixed two plates of eggs, tortillas, and fried beans without ever looking to see if her nephew's newest bride was happy.

Lindano devoured his eggs. Mary was scared, but not

heartbroken, and she did not see how she would ever free herself of Lindano if she starved herself. She was well mounted and a better horseman than Lindano. She had decided to try and keep herself sound and watch for the moment when she could jump Steeldust out ahead of Little Pie, outride Lindano's sore butt, and escape. She ate a good breakfast.

Lindano tied Mary, laid her on his uncle's bed, lay down beside her, let out a long, sighing moan, and slept. Later, in his sleep, he nuzzled her back with his big, snuffling nose. She cringed, but did not jump away. She knew she would have to submit to a lot more than a snuffle without having a fit if she were to survive. She did not have to give up her life. When the time came, she would have to burn horseflesh to get away from him, but she wanted to be aboard Steeldust. One jump on Steeldust was all she needed to lay dust on the whole damned country. She did not care how many Mexicans Lindano recruited to come after her.

Mary had been close to death and suffering all her life. She had fought it with Bill, Tom, her mother and father, and the animals they nursed. She had watched suffering closely. She had not suffered, but she believed she would be able to follow the example of the brave and show courage when her time came. She had been telling Bill she was ready for her trials as a woman. Her rampages had certainly been valorous enough. She now had a chance to take on her own trial with dignity.

Lindano awakened at nightfall and jumped off the bed in a rush. He untied Mary as hurriedly as he would untie a horse that he had forgotten to feed and water. He rubbed her wrists and ankles, grabbed her by the hair, and pulled back her head to look into her face. The truth was, as a coward, Lindano feared Mary. He could not look her in the eye because he dreaded seeing her contempt. He could not let her anger him because she was goods, and he must not damage her if he was to use her in a trade. He had no intention of riling her until he could have her at his secret place. When he decided to take hold of her flesh, she would not have time to think of anything but her own disgrace, and even then he would not be able to look Mary in the eye. He left the room. Mary went to listen at the door.

"Mahout, the horses have been fed, but the little horse you ride won't eat," the uncle was saying.

"The big horse is the one we must keep healthy. The others don't matter."

"And the child? What will you do with her?"

"What child? That child in there is much of a woman. You don't know her the way I do. I have to tie her so she'll leave me alone when I'm trying to rest."

"What a man," the uncle said, as though he were flattering Lindano. "You always have an eye for a good horse, a pretty woman, and a quick profit. Where will you go from here?" The uncle was mocking Lindano. He knew Lindano had slept as soundly as an ox at ploughing time, but flattery might get the uncle another gold piece.

"South. Is Pascual still at the Molino Rojo?"

"Yes. The American had a fever, but is recovering. Pascual got drunk watching over him."

"The American? What American? I thought I killed the American."

"The one you shot is still alive."

"Bah! Bill Shane with a whole gizzard? And Zuni?"

"Ah, you killed Zuni."

"The gringo Shane lives? I shot him in the head and only gave him a fever? Are you sure?"

"Hah, don't I clean under his bed every day? You only scratched his head. You hit him hard in the shoulder and leg, though. He can't walk or throw rocks, but he talks, laughs, and gives me big tips. Is Steeldust the name of the big horse the girl is riding?"

"That's him, the horse I was telling you about. What do you think of him, Uncle?"

"He's a Señor horse, all right. He's already famous here."

"How is that, Uncle?"

"The radio is talking about him."

"The radio?"

"The radio from Tucson says he was stolen when the girl was kidnapped. The horse is famous wherever a Sonoran or Arizonan listens to the radio."

"Who do they say stole the horse and kidnapped the girl?"

"Your name is often mentioned in that respect. You were seen by the girl's mother."

"Well, the horse and the girl are mine now, and there are no radios where I'm taking them. Have Bill Shane and Pascual heard the report?"

"I doubt it. The music of the mariachis is loud in the Molino Rojo. When those two aren't with the mariachis, they're asleep."

Mary heard Lindano coming toward her and she recoiled. He opened the door and came after her. He took her by the back of the neck and forced her out of the house.

"We're going for a walk, Miss Mary," he said. "We're going to visit a sick friend. Did you know you had a sick friend here?"

Lindano kept Mary ahead of him as he moved through the alleys to the Molino Rojo. He stopped outside the light of a window. Bill and Pascual were drinking mescal and laughing at a table inside. Their hats were on the backs of their heads. Bill's wounded leg was propped on a chair. The medicine of mescal was keeping it comfortable. One arm was in a sling. Lindano aimed his pistol at Bill's face. He squeezed Mary's mouth to keep her quiet. He smiled at Bill through his secret gunsight.

Pascual laid his head on the table. Bill was smiling at the window, straight at Mary, but she was out of the light and he could not see her. Lindano smiled back at Bill, turned Mary's face to his, slobbered a kiss on her mouth, and faced her back to Bill. A whore walked up to the table, cocked her hip, and nudged Pascual. Bill laughed.

Lindano let his own mirth sound in his throat. Bill looked at the window and sobered. Lindano laughed out loud. Bill scrambled from his chair, trying to stand. The chair spilled him on the floor. Lindano yelled and mocked him and ran Mary back to his uncle's house.

Placido Matus was squatting in the deep-night shadow across the alley from Lindano. This was his station for watching and waiting for his father. When Lindano left the alley with Mary, Placido picked up the morral with his possibles, his gourd *bule* for his water, and his machete, and he followed them.

Lindano packed Copper with his bed and provision, and tied Copper's lead to Steeldust's tail. He loaded Mary on her horse, mounted, and left his uncle's house without even a good-bye. His aunt and uncle did not follow him out to wave to him, either.

Lindano laughed to himself. The girl would never outrun him with a pack-horse tied to Steeldust's tail. At a high point above the town, he stopped and listened for pursuit, and none came. He screamed over the town with ringing yips of triumph, and then he led Mary off into the darkness toward the south.

Lindano began to rejoice in having Mary, for the pleasure she would give him. His marrow swelled, and his bones softened with lust when he thought of it. So far, he had not detached even a hair from her head. Once he began indulging himself, he would not be able to stop, he was afraid. He never opened a bottle of good wine without drinking it all in one sitting.

He began planning every step of his ravishment of Mary to keep his mind off the pain of his ride. A plan would help him keep his temper when it came time to deal with her defenses. She was not big enough to hurt him, but if she submitted quickly because she could not endure pain, or conflict, he would be angered. He knew how to push her to the edge of meanness so she could give him the response he enjoyed. Such was his finesse with women.

If Mary fought with all her instinct, his joy would be in quelling her. That was always the best part, quelling the beautiful fierceness, twisting the shapely arm he had made fierce, changing the look in the clean, bright eye. The pure eyes would eventually cloud with his use. He would ruin the straight line of Mary's nose, put his own signature on her face, create a new demeanor to take the place of the one God had given her. He had his own place on the edge of the world for that business.

Like all cowards, Lindano tried to live with his cowardice by bragging to himself about it. He hated being cowardly, but loved it when his cowardice kept him safe, or comfortable, or brought him pleasure. He was respectful of Mary's decency and afraid of being caught in the act of hurting her. He was terrified his meanness would inspire the same meanness in the man who might catch him at it.

He was also afraid of another great adversary, the child's innocence. Innocence humiliated him, and Mary was completely pure, but sooner or later the child would have to do something mean to him to save herself. When she turned mean, Lindano would be able to take her in his grip. Then her innocence would desert her. At present, even the look in her eye distracted him.

By daylight, Lindano and Mary were on San Bernardino Pass looking down on the Rio Sonora. He pushed the horses along the river all day. In the evening, they approached the town of Milpita, and Little Pie was staggering with fatigue. Milpita was a pueblo where drovers with herds and pack trains congregated. Lindano stopped at a hotel and livery. The liveryman walked around Little Pie, examining him.

"You came a long way in a short time," the liveryman said.

"True," Lindano said.

"A hard way. This horse is finished. Your little girl is tired, too. Allow my wife to attend to her."

"For a liveryman, you don't know much about horses. We can travel another five days before we'll require rest or a change of horses."

"A lot of horses come through here. This is a country of tough horses. I'm telling you, ease up on the little sorrel and the girl, or don't stop here. Why don't you ride the big sorrel and go on alone? Leave the little ones here to rest."

"We won't require much from you. We'll have supper, sleep the night, and be gone in the morning."

"I've heard of this horse the girl is riding. So has everybody in the state of Sonora."

"I doubt it, unless you've been in the United States lately."

"This is the horse called Steeldust, the one the radio announces. This is the missing girl. You are Mahout Lindano, and you're wanted for questioning for a murder in Arizona."

"Wanted? Who wants me? You know me. I was here with the cavalry only a few months ago. Do you want me? I'm on my way to the garrison at Sahuaripa. I'm working for the government, as always. I want food and shelter for myself, the girl, and the horses. I'll pay with the usual government note."

"Yes, I know you and who you work for and how much your *vales*, your notes, are worth. We all know you here."

"That's right, you know me. I never hide. What kind of trouble are you trying to make for me?"

"No kind of trouble, nothing. Go and rest. My hotel and restaurant are yours. The child can stay with my woman."

"The child stays with me. If the sorrel is still tired in the morning, I'll have to take one of your horses."

"Are you joking, man? You are the one with the horses. We are with burros. Horses are gold."

"Feed my horses. I'll pay. Give them corn."

"Listen, I feed every horse that stops here. I love horses."

"Sure, you love horses, but you really love gold."

"I would love to know that the pile of *vales* I have accumulated in my desk would someday be paid—even with paper money," the liveryman said as Lindano led Mary away.

Lindano put Mary in a room in the hotel. He sat down in a place in its small restaurant where he could have a drink and watch her door. The windows in the room were barred with iron, as was the custom.

The liveryman was in the restaurant with the cattle inspector of the region. They did not look at Lindano. Lindano knew the inspector. The inspector was a leader of a faction that could harm him. In Sonora the military held the power. The Government was occupied with trying to exterminate the Yaquis, and as an agent of the cavalry, Lindano was protected. Civil law in the unpopulated regions was enforced by the ranchers. The organized crews of cattlemen that rode against thieves and murderers were called *La Cordada*. They were under the authority of the governor of the state, who had little authority otherwise. They hung horse or cattle thieves wherever they could catch them. They applied the "law of flight" to murderers and kidnappers by allowing them to run for freedom across the open plain while they used them for target practice. Thieves were never allowed to live if they were caught by *La Cordada*.

Lindano bought a liter *amphora* of tequila. The inspector was listening to a long, intense story the liveryman was telling him. Lindano was sure the story was about him. He went back to the room, tied Mary to the bed, lay down beside her, and slept.

Little Pie was suffering. His legs ached, so he could not stand still. Steeldust was aware of his suffering and stayed close to him. He switched Little Pie's face with his tail to keep away the mosquitos. Little Pie was too tired to reciprocate. Finally, he was able to comfort himself by leaning against Steeldust's side. He slept. A half hour later Lindano and Mary walked into the corral.

Lindano rode along the Sonora River all the rest of the night. Mary slept in the saddle. At daylight he approached a ranch. A man was turning his milk cows out to pasture. Mary watched him carry two foaming pails of milk down a trail, out of sight. Little Pie fell when Lindano dismounted at the corral. Lindano stomped him until he stood up again, then unsaddled him, and penned him in the rancher's fodder bin.

Little Pie laid himself down, rolled over on his side, and began grinding his teeth. Lindano hated him and did not care that he was finished. He led Copper to a shady pen by a water trough and fed him. He tied Steeldust in the sun and gave him nothing. He tied Mary and lay down in the fodder bin and slept. He awoke sweating at midday with the sun on his face. He ate a lunch of jerky and *pinole,* gave some to Mary, and slept again. Steeldust was still tied in the sun.

At sundown, Lindano put his saddle on Steeldust, mounted him, and reined him to start him. The horse did not move. Lindano coaxed him with his spurs, but he did not respond. Lindano bounced his spurs off his sides. The horse flinched, but moved not a hoof. He turned his head so he could look at Lindano, then looked straight ahead and worked his ears as if to inquire, "Could it be he wants something worthwhile?" He waited for Lindano to do the right thing and dismount and go away. Lindano sliced his chain quirt across the horse's flanks. Steeldust sprang away, dropped his head beneath the earth's crust, kicked high behind, shook his hide, and rigidly pounded his feet. He stood on his hind feet, twisted, kicked and struck at the sky, and somersaulted Lindano to the ground on his head. Mary laughed for Steeldust in a high, clear voice.

"That's just fine," said Lindano. He stood up and staggered a step. To Mary, his eyes seemed to have been brought closer together by his contact with the ground and she rolled over on her side, helpless with laughter. Lindano trotted lamely after the horse. His hat was crumpled on his head. "I gave you your chance," he said. "Now, you'll see what I can do to you."

He caught Steeldust and tied all four feet together. He pulled Steeldust's head around. The horse lunged and fell on his side. Lindano held him there and began beating him with the quirt. Mary screamed. Lindano looked up and saw a packtrain crossing the river. The drovers had stopped to water their horses and were watching him. Lindano shouted to them and a drover rode toward him so he could hear him over the sound of the river.

"Do you have a horse for sale?" yelled Lindano. He knew the drover. The drovers had probably been listening to the radio, as had everyone else in the state.

"Let that one up and use him, why don't you?" asked the drover.

"I'm not asking what to do with this horse. I need another horse, that's all," Lindano said, smiling.

"Come to our camp and we'll talk." The drover had not looked at Mary. "We'll be upriver. We'll trade you out of the horse and the girl, lighten your troubles." He rode to catch up with his companions.

Lindano turned back to Steeldust. The rancher was standing at the corral gate with his milk cows. Lindano opened the gate to let the cows in.

"My cows strayed," the rancher said. He only glanced at Steeldust, but he looked squarely into Mary's white face.

"I wondered when you were coming back," said Lindano to the rancher. "I owe you for some horse feed."

"You don't owe me anything," said the rancher. He looked carefully at Steeldust, then at Mary again, exacting his own payment for the feed. "I've been a traveler and good people have sheltered me and fed my horses. You can pay me by untying that horse on the ground and letting him up, so he can walk to the shade and drink. How did the other horse die?"

"Is he dead? I thought he was just resting."

"Yes, he's resting. Forever. In a pen without water. Was he sick?"

"He was old, poor horse. Poor Little Pie. Do you have a team of horses to drag him away so he won't stink?"

"Only mules."

"I'll pay you to do it."

"No matter. And this one on the ground? Do you want me to drag him away, too? He'll die there, sweating and grunting like that."

"He's too stubborn to die."

"A beautiful horse. A shame when men like me and you are allowed to get our hands on a fine horse. We always find fault with him. He's too active for us, or walks too slow, or groans too loud when we tie him down, or is too stubborn to die when we are trying to kill him."

"This one was given me by a man who had no use for him. He may be of no use to me, either."

"Or, he becomes of no use to us. . . . According to the radio, a horse of this description was recently stolen from an American. The thief will probably find out the horse can be of no use to him, either, because the horse is now also too well known, don't you think?"

"Oh?" Lindano narrowed his eyes at the rancher and whipped his own leg with the quirt.

"Yes, I heard the horse was stolen by a man named Lindano, who is also well known in this region. This Lindano also kidnapped a rancher's daughter. This Lindano is a poison who often comes to this region."

The rancher watched Lindano calmly.

"I'll tell you," said Lindano. "Anyone who would steal this horse is a fool. This horse is worthless." He stroked Steeldust's eye with the popper on his quirt. Steeldust lay in torment, holding his breath as long as he could, then releasing it in a long groan.

"Why do you tie him down?" asked the rancher. "What do you do with him when he's down like that?"

"When I tied him he was standing. To be in accord with himself he threw himself down. He lies there and groans because he wants to." Lindano laughed.

"*Que bruto!*" said the rancher. "What a brute!" He turned his back on Lindano and walked away.

Lindano beat Steeldust until he tired of it. He spared only the horse's eyes. He walked away to sit and cool down. He built a fire, made himself coffee, and carefully fed himself. He kept his eyes on the fire, his attention on his repast. He had to make himself whole. He was still afoot.

At nightfall, he tied Mary to his wrist and went back into the corral. He stood over Steeldust and raised the quirt to strike again. A movement distracted him. Placido, son of Pascual Matus, was walking toward him balancing a broad machete in his hands. Lindano reached for his pistol. Mary jerked him off balance with the rope on her wrist to keep him from taking aim. Placido swung the blade at Lindano's head. Lindano deflected it with the pistol, and the flat side of the blade rang off his head. He lost sight of the boy. The blade rang off the rope on his wrist, and Mary sprang free and ran away. Lindano ran to catch her, stopped, and raised the pistol to shoot her.

"Look at you, Lindano," someone said.

Lindano turned. The rancher was outside the corral pointing his rifle at Lindano. "I wish my friend Bill Shane was here to use that chain quirt on you," he said.

Lindano walked toward the rancher. The rancher let him come on to keep him from the boy and girl.

"Don't kill me," said Lindano.

"I won't have to," said the rancher. "*La Cordada* is on its way here to hang you."

Lindano stooped through the fence, came up under the rifle, butted the rancher, and knocked him down. The rancher tried to bring the rifle to bear on Lindano again.

Lindano looked into his eyes and shot him. He walked to his side and kicked the rifle away. He mounted Copper bareback and rode away from the corrals. Then, he circled in the brush and rode back. He found Placido and Mary trying to help the rancher. Lindano reloaded his pistol. Copper churned and roiled beneath him. He looked up again, but Mary and Placido were not in sight.

Lindano circled the corrals, looking for them, and watching for their tracks. He found Mary, sitting under an alamo tree, watching him. He grinned at her and rode to the tree.

A shadow fell across him, and Copper shied quickly away. Lindano looked up just as he was struck a weak blow on the top of his head. Copper's shying had saved him from being beheaded. Placido was hanging in the tree, just out of reach now, waving his machete at Lindano's head. Then, Copper spun and reared as Placido jumped to the horse's hips, behind Lindano. Placido grappled with Lindano, screamed in his ear, and stabbed at him with his machete. Copper pitched and brushed Placido off against a tree, and Lindano ran him on out of sight.

The drovers rode up to the corrals with the cattle inspector. Copper's dust was just settling. In a hurry to be after Lindano, the inspector stopped only long enough to see that Mary was attending to the rancher. Then, he and the drovers rode away tracking Lindano.

Placido and Mary were alone again. He stood up over the rancher. "We must go," he said.

"No, what about this poor man? He'll die."

"He's dead," Placido said. He untied Steeldust and let him up. He led him to water, rubbed him, took off Lindano's saddle and saddled him with Mary's saddle. He motioned to Mary. "Mount your horse," he said.

"No, the men will be back. We have to tell them about Lindano. They'll want to take me home."

"Lindano will be back. We can't stay here."

Mary mounted and moved her foot out of the stirrup so Placido could ride behind her.

"Let's go," Placido said and walked away.

"Aren't you going to ride?" Mary asked.

"Oooooooo," said Placido derisively. He believed he could outwalk any horse alive in the rock and brush and mountains, and he knew every step in daylight or dark to his grandmother's ranch in the Sierra Madre.

CHAPTER 4

Most of mankind knows nothing about a mule. Mules are secretive, and man can seldom learn anything about them. A mule is half ass and half horse, and perhaps therein lies the root of his complexity. He is a hybrid and unable to procreate. This gives him an inordinate sense of self-preservation and a selfish cunning.

No matter how much a man may learn about a mule, he is always astounded by the mule's propensity for evil. The mule is wonderfully inventive of new mischief he can perpetrate on man. If it is true the Devil cannot possess a good horse, it is also true an idle mule harbors demons in his heart.

LINDANO was afraid of machetes. The prospect of being hacked, disfigured, or dismembered by a machete in the hands of a Yaqui caused him to run away in panic. He was a vain man. The loss of his finger still caused a big tear to form in his eye. He was also afraid of *La Cordada*. The men in *La Cordada* were worse than Apaches. They were supposed to be Christians, but they enjoyed the spectacle of execution more even than Apaches.

The men of *La Cordada* would not hesitate even long enough to get off their horses before they hanged Lindano, now that he had shot one of their ranchers. They would not grant him even the privilege of the law of flight. He needed to hurry and join the cavalry, but he did not have much of a horse to ride. If *La Cordada* did not catch him and kill him, Copper might do it. He was afraid of the horse. He had long been able to see that Copper wanted to kill any man who used him. Lindano had always thought the horse was a dark sorrel, but the more he looked at him, the more he saw black. The horse was turning black. Why had that runt Jonas named him Copper? The horse was tarnishing because of an evil change of season inside him, no doubt.

That Yaqui had been in position to hack off his ear, both ears, or his nose. If Copper had not gone wild when the Yaqui jumped on him, Lindano's whole head might still be twitching in the dust by the corral.

Nevertheless, Lindano tried to ride Copper hard enough to kill him. He wanted the horse to be dead when he reached the garrison. He never wanted to have to look at Copper again. Copper paid him back by using a gait that twisted his spine. He never walked a nice, slow walk. He kept jigging in place until Lindano let him trot. Then, when he trotted, his naked backbone sawed at Lindano's sore tail. He loped as though he had five anvils on his feet. Then, when Lindano gave him his head and let him run, Copper was so reckless, he gave Lindano a good look into his own grave. The more tired Copper became, the higher he carried his head and the less he watched where he was going. He was hard to hold. He stepped suicidally close to the edges of the precipices. He plunged through the thickets. He stumbled over ditches and holes. When the garrison finally came in sight, Lindano made a headlong rush for the gate. He hated the horse so much he handed him over to the sentry to be shot.

"Be merciful and shoot this poor horse for me, sentry," Lindano said. "I've ridden him to death." He tried to show a mask of concern for the horse. He knew the best tool for murder in Mexico was any little, brown, southern *guacho* sentry like this one who had probably joined the army because he had murdered someone at home.

This sentry was a native of Jalisco, a Zapotec Indian who knew tough horses. The look of suffering on Lindano's face was pitiful. The sentry knew what a coward he was. He turned and inspected the horse and saw why Lindano was afraid to kill him. The horse was the kind that had the look in his eye that a soldier wished on his enemy.

"*Vaya.* Go bury yourself," the sentry said. "The horse has finished you and done an able service, and he remains sound. He'll run you into your grave before he draws a long breath from a ride you make on him. I'll shoot you, though, if you wish."

Bill had been trying to sober up since he heard Lindano's voice laughing at him outside the saloon. Pascual was still drunk. Bill still thought Mary and Steeldust were safe at Red Rock, but the impact of bullets had dimmed his memory of loves and duties. Since he had been shot, he had not enjoyed a moment in which he was fully conscious.

Every morning he woke up enough to suggest to Pascual that they stay sober long enough to leave, but he made the mistake of drinking with Pascual while they talked. Each afternoon he gave up to drink again. Each night he caroused shamelessly.

One morning he found himself awake and, by the grace of God, sober, though still buried in a whorehouse. Pascual was on the floor with his head against the wall, his chin on his chest, snoring. Bill tried to rise off the bed. The door banged open, and Tom Ford walked in.

"Look at you. I wish you could see yourself," Tom said. "You look pitiful."

"I was just trying to get my head out from under me, again," Bill said.

"Partner, it's time for you to get moving."

"I know you're sure of that, and I know it's damned important, but I can't remember any good reason for it. I been on the painkiller pretty heavy. I like it, too."

"I suppose you're gonna tell me you don't know Lindano's been to Red Rock and stole your horse and girl."

"Lindano stole *what?*"

"Hell, Bill. It's on the radio. Every cowpuncher in the Southwest is out looking for them. Do you mean to tell me you're the only one don't know it?"

"Know what, goddammit?"

"Lindano kidnapped Mary. We tracked him here. He's taken her south."

"No, goddammit. I was afraid that sonofabitch would come back."

"Bill, wake up. Your horse has been stolen, and your girl's been kidnapped by a damned pervert."

"Well, let's go get him," Bill said angrily.

"Yes, by God. You get up and get going. You've been killing the pain too long, now. Time to let it come on and hurt a little."

"Huh! You ought to get shot. You wouldn't be so full of yourself. A forty-five slug knocks you down, kills you, and buries you. A slug that big knocks more out of a man than just his wind, I'll guarandamtee you."

"Well, you haven't been gutshot, so you don't have to stay down with your tail in the air like a stink bug. Get up."

"Wake up the Yaqui, then. You try it. Maybe you can get him moving. He can get going after Lindano right now, if Lindano's in Mexico. Let him go. I'm tired of looking at him. I'll sober up, and let myself heal a little longer, and maybe I can ride out of here about next week."

"Up with you, up. Your only trouble is in your gizzard. You've lost your sand. Get up and get to pecking around. Pretty soon you'll be crowing again. Nobody's going after your horse and your woman but you. You were so bound and determined to settle down with just one horse and one woman. Well, get after them. It's time to get moving."

Tom jerked the covers off Bill. The sight of the leg stunned him. Bill kept the bandages off now. The sight of the maroon thigh with a hole healing in it stopped Tom. He rolled Bill over and looked at the other side where the slug had come out. The thigh looked as though it had been dynamited. Tom turned away and kicked the soles of Pascual's huaraches.

"Wake up, Pascual," Tom said. "No more sleeping."

An hour later, Bill and Pascual were mounted and headed south. Tom had gone back to the herd. Pascual was riding his dun mare mule, La Loca. Bill was riding Lizard. Before he passed the last house on the edge of Fronteras, Bill felt he could not ride another step. Lizard had the roughest trot in the world. Pascual did not pull up for three days.

At Milpita, a lieutenant of *La Cordada* told them Lindano had made it to the garrison at Bacanora alone. Mary and Placido had been seen together headed into the *Sierra Oscura* of the Sierra Madre, the highest, darkest mountains southeast of Milpita, two hundred miles away.

Pascual headed for his mother's ranch at Canelas in the Sierra. He was sure Placido and Mary would be there if nothing happened to them, or he would find them along the way. He decided it was time to look his enemies in the face again, and he knew where he could find them. A troop of cavalry was already bivouacked there. Intent on this, he seldom looked back to see if Bill was keeping up.

Bill knew he would never see Mary's face again unless he kept riding. He also knew he would not be much good in a fight because he hurt so much. He could not help but wish that he could lie down and expire in peace, but Pascual kept going, and he kept following.

A day and a half south of Milpita, Bill quit. The sooner he rested, the sooner he could start making a real hand in his search for Mary. He was in such misery that he stopped Lizard, dismounted, and stretched himself out on the ground in the sun.

After a while Pascual stopped, came back, and stood La Loca over Bill's head. Bill's eyes were closed. "Pascual," he said. "I can't ride this horse, with these wounds opening and closing with every step. We have fifty leagues to go, and we've come fifty, and I couldn't fight a blowfly off my beans.''

Pascual stepped off his mule and unsaddled Lizard. He put his own saddle on Lizard and put Bill's saddle on La Loca. He said, "We'll go on a little farther before we camp. You can lie in a cold stream awhile before you sleep. For now, we'll have a drink of mescal. Your trouble is, you haven't had a drop to kill your pain in five days. I'm dying for a drink to rest my mule, myself. You're despairing, not because of your wounds, but because you got used to the medicine in the mescal and you cut it off. It's time we had mercy on ourselves. Let's have a few swallows, rest awhile, then you can ride my crazy mule and enjoy a smooth mount.''

Pascual brought out a bottle of mescal he had been carrying in his morral and handed it to Bill. Bill uncorked it, took a fat swallow, then another, and immediately felt better.

"Tonight, I'll doctor your leg and shoulder, Bill. If we can put some life into it, you'll be able to ride La Loca the rest of the way without pain. She's the finest trail mule I ever saw, and she's homing in on my mother's ranch where she's been fed corn like a queen all her life. She's my mother's own mount. I know you can make it. Of all the men I know, I can't see you stopping here and giving up the ghost on a bed of rocks. This is no place to die, but I might let you die at Canelas. Now, take another swallow. Let it settle. That's all you need, you'll see, a little swallow of the *fuerte,* the strong stuff.''

Bill began to come to life. Pascual was right. He did not need to lay down his bones in this barren place. He just had not been conscious of anything but pain for a long time.

He moved into the shade and sat with his back against the trunk of a mesquite. He sighed and took another swallow of mescal.

After a while he dragged his body aboard La Loca. Pascual spurred Lizard down the trail and did not look back again until dark. Bill did not mind. The mescal smoothed the trail for him, and La Loca mothered him along. He just sat on the mule and traveled. She had a great, running walk—probably a famous one—but no other gait. She was geared to carry an invalid, or an old lady, but Lord help Bill Shane if anyone attacked him. The mule was just a one-gaited old thing with her sights on home, but Bill was comfortable at last.

"Why didn't you put me on this mule in Fronteras and save me all of Lizard's torture," Bill asked Pascual one day.

"I didn't know you'd give up riding one of your precious horses for a mule. You brag that you'll never loan your pistol, your horse, or your woman. Who was I to cross you? You say mules can't run with racehorses. Who was I to put you on a mule? Remember, she's just a mule, so don't fall in love with her. She's not comforting you to save your life. She's being nice so she can tear your wounds open when you least suspect it. She's a mule."

Lindano went into the *Cuartel* to report to Captain Echeverria. The Captain was working at his desk and did not raise his head to look at him. He was never glad to see Lindano, but he always needed horses. He decided he could endure the return of an old chancre once more if he brought horses. He looked up from his papers.

Lindano's hat was crammed down on his head. Blood encrusted his face. His shirt was torn and filthy. He stood hipshot to rest his tortured backbone, and his trousers made a bag that hung on one hip.

"What sort of trouble have you brought me this time, Mahout?" the captain asked. "Look at your shabby carcass. I can imagine the quality of the horses you brought."

"This time I brought only the mount that carried me, Captain," Lindano said. "I was in such a hurry to bring you news that I came bareback, riding only the hair of my mount."

"Please do not begin to explain the reasons you came

bareback. I know them all. You are always being forced to mount the hair of a beast in haste. What sort of horse did you ride here?"

"A rabid, black one, with red in his eye, and a gait that leaves a man with a twisted spine."

"What bloodline?"

"Ah, he's from the good Bradford horses."

"You brought me the horse called Steeldust?"

"No, but he's from the same stock."

"Where is Steeldust, then, the stud horse that has been making you infamous on the radio, the horse you stole with the Bradford girl?"

"Imagine, Captain, the girl slipped away from me on that horse."

"Bah!" the captain said. He laughed. "You stole a horse, and a *gringita* took him away from you?"

"They haven't escaped, Captain. I know where they are. Give me a small troop and I'll bring them right back."

"You need my cavalry to overcome a *gringita*? You expect to use my troops to chase after an innocent girl? You pervert. If it weren't for the palomino horse you gave me, the horse I most esteem, my companion of rigorous campaign, I would stand you against the wall and shoot you.

"*La Cordada* is asking to be remembered to you. I have supported you in the past because you brought me horses. Now you return with only one shabby horse, and a whole population of good people pursuing you. Give me up for dead. This time I won't give you asylum. *La Cordada* awaits you outside my gate. If those Sonora gentlemen even say one disapproving word to me I'm going to give you to them. I have no reason to keep you."

"You do, Captain. I can give you Placido, son of Matus. He is with the girl and I know where they are."

"Where, Mahout?"

"They're on their way to Canelas, I'm sure of it. Pascual Matus, the old savage himself, will be there, too, now that propaganda is being spread over the radio. This is your chance to capture him. I've lured the whole tribe back to the Yaqui from points you would never dream they could stray."

The captain watched Lindano a moment. "Yes," he said. "You're sure Matus will be at Canelas?"

"Believe me, Pascual won't be far behind his son and the girl. The *buquis* are both riding Steeldust. The weight of two children can easily kill a horse. Pascual will catch up to them, and so will we. Canelas is the only place they can be headed. The Yaqui boy will wait there for his father."

"The girl is a prize in herself. All right. Tell me," the captain said.

"We don't have to hurry, and we can probably catch them at La Escondida, the ranch of the gringo Cabezón. We can stage the capture from there, if you like. Placido Matus can't hide that horse, or that girl's blue eyes, anywhere in Sonora. Placido won't rest or eat this side of La Escondida. We might catch him there."

The Captain pulled on his gloves, went to his mirror, and set his barracks hat in place over his eyes. He strapped on his saber and pistol and called in his orderly.

"Draw rations and clothing for this man," he ordered. "Draw him a bridle, blankets, and saddle. Ready a patrol for a week's march. I want to be gone from here within the hour."

"But look at me, Captain," said Lindano. "I have to rest. These children can't outdistance us now. We can leave tomorrow and catch them easily. I've not rested in days, in *months*. I've worked hard luring these people here. Anyway, what would I ride? The horse I rode here is nearly dead with fatigue."

"Precisely. You'll draw rations and bless anew the ghost you've been riding. You'll sleep on horseback until you've rested. You'll stand at parade within the hour, or rest on the cutting edge of my saber."

An hour later, Lindano was aboard Copper and headed away from bed and board, with Copper's vengeful trot bending his bones again.

Placido, Mary, and Steeldust took the trail for La Escondida that day at the same time Captain Echeverria's troop left the *Cuartel* at Bacanora. On the way, Placido stopped with a relative and dressed Mary in loose, white cotton trousers, and the blouse, sash, and headband of a Yaqui boy. He gave her leather-thonged huaraches for her feet. He dirtied her feet and face with mud he made from sifted dust. He cautioned her to keep her eyes narrowed so they would not shine blue out of the mud and surprise the people.

Mary felt that she was part of the country now, and part of old Steeldust. She had always felt close to her father's land and livestock. Now she felt that cactus, rock, dust, and meager sweat were her allies. Steeldust never faltered. She knew she would make it home. She liked the trail that God had given her to travel. She had faced the real Devil and she might not have beaten him, but at least he had run away. She knew she should be headed north to her folks, but Placido thought the best way to escape was south where they could avoid all *Yoris,* whites. He felt the *Yoris* were waiting to trap them in the north. The *Yoris* could sell them for a wealth of ransom at a time when almost nothing else in Sonora was worth a cent. Because of Placido's relations with the people and the country, he had kept the three of them strong, well fed, and rested.

In the late afternoon, on a point above Rancho La Escondida, Placido climbed a rock to study the country. Only two trails converged at the ranch. One from the west and one from the north. Evening was a bad time for a Yaqui to ride in on a ranch. Ranchers were hospitable to everyone, and an unwary Yaqui might find a cavalry sergeant in the bed he had hoped to use.

Placido saw the dust of horses coming on his back trail. If

he did not go in to La Escondida, the only other trail left to him was the one toward the garrison at Bacanora. Placido and Mary had time to eat and water at La Escondida and go on before the men on their back trail reached the ranch. No strange horses were in the corrals at the ranch. Placido started down off the rock. Then he heard metal rattle in a canyon below him on the Bacanora trail. He watched awhile and saw Lindano lead a troop of cavalry across an open space climbing toward the ranch. The only avenue left Placido was to beat the cavalry to the ranch and hide there. He could not hide Mary and Steeldust on the trail.

Placido mounted Steeldust with Mary and hurried off the mountain to the ranch while the troop was still in the canyon. He ran Steeldust past the corrals and outbuildings, through the wide door of a warehouse that adjoined the main house, past stacks of ranch stores, and into a pantry off the kitchen. He closed the pantry door, and he and Mary and Steeldust stood in absolute darkness, breathing the tart odors of dried fruits and cinnamon. The darkness quieted Steeldust's feet, but his breathing was heavy, and the sound of his pounding heart made Mary laugh.

"*¿Que es esto?* What is this?" someone asked. The door to the kitchen opened, and a large woman stared into the pantry.

"*Miramiramira,* a horse the size of a mastodon, and blue eyes in the face of a Yaqui. Am I in a dream? *Patrón,* come and see." The woman began to laugh.

The Texas hardtwist known as Cabezón "Bighead" Woodell came and looked into his pantry. Les Woodell had come to Sonora looking for country for his cattle. He had decided to stay in the country of the Yaquis. He was small, hard and neat as rawhide, fair and blue-eyed. He was called Bighead for the big Texas hat he wore. He knew the Matus boy, and he looked into Mary's eyes and recognized her resemblance to his childhood friend, R.E. Bradford. He owned a radio. Every day for the past week he had dispatched cowboys to look for Mary. He had been watching for her and was not in the least surprised to see her.

"That must be a big, hungry pack of hounds that run you into my chuck box," said Cabezón.

Placido and Mary moved into the kitchen. The woman started to lead the horse out of her pantry into the warehouse.

"No, Margara," said Cabezón. "The government is probably out there." He bolted the door to the warehouse, led Steeldust back into the farthest corner of the pantry, and closed and locked the door to the kitchen. "How close are the *guachitos*?" he asked Placido.

"They're here," Placido said and with that someone rapped on the door. Cabezón climbed on the kitchen table, lifted Mary and Placido onto a beam, and handed each of them a baking-soda biscuit. The beam was wide enough to hide them. He opened the door and admitted Captain Echeverria, Lindano, and a sergeant known as El Bordado. The sergeant was called "The Embroidered One" for the seams of scars that held his face together.

The captain removed his gloves while he searched and sniffed at the odors in the kitchen.

"You're well escorted this time, Captain," said Cabezón. "This must not be a routine patrol."

"Matus's son is coming here. We suspect Matus himself is coming back," the Captain said, looking down his nose.

"Before I arm myself and all my people and barricade my door, let Margara serve you coffee, biscuits, and wild honey," said Cabezón. "You're on dangerous patrol. The biscuit is the bread of the Texan and will help you with your heroic work. Bivouack your troops here. Use my barns, corrals, and feed bins. Draw from my food stores and firewood. Be at home. Is this Lindano? I recognize you. I hear awful stories about you. I see they can't be true because you're here with your captain. Can they be true?"

The captain was searching the kitchen with a cautious

glitter in his eye. He was used to taking what he wanted but was unsure of himself with Cabezón. The Texan's neighbor was Colonel Maytorena of La Misa, the captain's superior. The colonel's hacienda was near La Escondida, and he and Cabezón were good friends.

Margara served the captain and his henchmen. The captain stared at her clean hands, bosoms, hips. He slurped his coffee and licked honey off his lips. He thanked her profusely for the repast and stared to see if she would smile at him. He might as well have been trying to get out from under her heel.

Mary had been holding the same bite of biscuit in her mouth since Lindano came into the room. She was afraid to chew it, or swallow it, afraid she would make a noise. The soda bread was delicious, and she craved to swallow it. The bread lay big, slick, and easy in her mouth. She sucked it longingly while it tried to make her swallow. She shifted it, and her jaws flexed. The morsel began to swell. She closed her eyes and tried to keep it still to stop the well of her saliva. She tried to think of something other than the biscuit so she would not have to swallow. Her jaws began to ache.

Lindano was standing beneath Mary, and he began to snuffle over his coffee. This tickled Mary with perverse and overpowering mirth. Laughter crowded the swollen biscuit in her mouth. She swallowed it whole, so she could breathe, and almost wept with horror and pain with the sound she made. She was having trouble holding her water, too. Then the tears started coming, and weeping began to crowd her dangerously. All she had wanted to do was lie quietly on top of the beam.

Lindano laid down his coffee cup and walked to the pantry door, guided by his senses. His senses knew the horse was in the pantry, that Placido and Mary were in the room. His senses were telling him his prey was within reach. The scent of the children lay strong in the room, with the bread and coffee, but he did not have the extra sense he needed to separate and identify the smells and tiny sounds. He tried the pantry door.

"No, that's not the way. The way out is through the other door. East," Margara said.

Lindano turned and smiled at her as though she had caressed him. "Thank you so much, Doña," he said, distracted. He walked out of the house with the captain and the sergeant, coveting Margara and wondering how her warm breasts would feel on his face.

The captain moved the troops up the trail toward Canelas that evening. Sensing the children had not passed Cabezón's ranch, Lindano doubled back, hid his tired horse by a spring overlooking Cabezón's barn, and waited. By morning, he knew Steeldust, Mary, and Placido were hiding there.

Bill and Pascual rode underneath the escarpment of Canelas to a pasture on the Río Yaqui. Pascual crowded a band of mules into a corner of the pasture and roped the first one that ran by him. He blindfolded and saddled the mule, threw the mantle of his leather *armas* over the saddlehorn, and turned Lizard loose with the mules. He mounted, and lifted the blindfold. The mule bucked all the way to the pasture gate, where she scared herself with an unnatural move, threw her head up, and quit. She blinked her eyes with surprise at the newest twists that had happened to her in her pitching. Pascual laughed at her.

"This mule is called *La Divorciada*—The Divorced Woman. "I am the only man in her life who has not spurned her. How do you like the way she bucks, *compadre?*"

"She bucks like a demon," Bill said. The long afternoon was wearing hard on him.

"Come on. Now we can ride to the ranch without worrying."

They climbed a trail beside the escarpment and stopped on a hill above the ranch. They saw a squad of cavalrymen pasturing horses in a meadow below the house.

"See why I left Lizard in the pasture?" asked Pascual. "He would have been scared on the cliffs. I don't worry about La Loca or La Divorciada. My mules are afraid for their own lives on the cliffs. The soldiers are confiscating horses and they can distinguish a horse from a mule at great distances. In this country a horse stands out like snow on a mountain. The soldiers don't bother us when they see us on mules. They know a man on horseback can't catch a mule in these mountains."

They watched Pascual's mother, Doña Juana, carry in some firewood. She did not seem to be much bothered or deterred by the soldiers.

"The first thing for us to do is let the *guachitos* see us," Pascual said. "Then we'll give them a taste of our medicine. When they're craving to kill us, we'll lead them away from here."

"I'm so sore I don't know how I'll help you get away," Bill said. "I'm sure to get caught. Don't pull anything for a while, *compadre*."

"We sure don't want them here, do we?" Pascual said. He rode off the hill and into a deep canyon that gave them cover and access to the ranch house. They stopped so close to the house they could hear Doña Juana scolding the soldiers and giving them a lecture on their manners. Pascual smiled at his mother's voice. He had been taught his catechism and his Christian table manners by her in that house.

"Look," Pascual said. He pointed back over his shoulder with his chin. A soldier stood on the edge of the canyon above them, examining their mules' tracks. He looked up and down the canyon, but avoided looking in the direction of Bill and Pascual.

"Why isn't he looking this way?" Bill asked. "He's already seen us, that's why. *Mierda*." He laughed.

"You're right," Pascual said. "He saw us."

"We'd better get the *la chingada* out of here, then."

"No, let's wait. Let's see what they do."

"I'll tell you what they'll do, Pascual. They'll just come in here and get us. We're in a box canyon and we can't get out if they come down the trail on our tracks."

"Let's wait. You take a little rest."

The soldier disappeared, and after a while he appeared at Doña Juana's house and went in. Doña Juana was feeding soldiers in her kitchen. A squad of cavalry rode in with Doña Juana's milk-cow drawn and quartered and draped in pieces over their saddles. One of the soldiers began salting the hide on the veranda. Another man carried the liver, heart, kidneys, paunch, and hooves into the kitchen for Doña Juana to cook in a *menudo*. The soldiers began slicing the meat into thin sheets, salting it, and hanging it along the veranda in the sun.

"We might have trouble bunching them together so they can all come after us at once," Pascual said. He laughed, and Bill was afraid the soldiers would hear him. Bill ached. His sweat was cooling on him without evaporating, and it made him cold. He wanted to measure his length on the ground. He looked up and saw Captain Echeverria riding toward the house with more cavalry. Bill took stock of his mule, *La Loca*. It was her carcass on which he hoped to flee, and she probably felt the same as he did about flight. He did not feel like running one step that day.

La Loca was not old, but she was too wise and cunning to be of any service to a man who needed to run for his life. In her youth she had probably learned the advantages of being ordinary when working with men. Now, she was in her prime, and wise to the success she enjoyed from being totally uncooperative. She had kept herself ordinary only in the physical attributes Bill needed. She was more like a burro in those attributes. When it came time for her to contribute courage, or speed, she would choke on the first full breath she had to take. Bill might as well have been riding a stick horse.

The sergeant known as El Bordado strutted out and

ordered the troops horseback. The captain rode to the head of the column and ordered it to wheel about for his review. Then he rode to the head of the column again and led it away from the ranch. Bill and Pascual climbed the side of the canyon to watch. The soldier who had seen them in the canyon broke ranks and rode up to speak to the captain. The captain nodded, wheeled the troops about again, and headed back toward the house.

"*¡Carajo!*" Pascual growled. "The *pinchi* soldier finally found the breath to tell on us."

To escape, Bill and Pascual had to ride out of the canyon, cross an open meadow to a pine forest, and run through a thick growth of jack pine back to a trail off the escarpment. No Mexican cavalryman would ever follow their mules off the cliffs of the escarpment.

The horses of the cavalrymen were exhausted and no match for Pascual's mules. Pascual was afraid of nothing. He would ride off those cliffs on *La Divorciada* with careless glee. Bill was bold when he was well-mounted; he could show the cavalry reckless, cowboy ways of sticking a mule off a cliff, but he knew *La Loca* was not going to hurry off any precipice for him. He wished he were riding Steeldust. Steeldust would sprout wings if Bill asked him to. *La Loca* thought too much of herself to do any flying for Bill.

The captain was ordering Doña Juana to tell him about the men his soldier had seen in the canyon.

"Just think of it, they're not here and I haven't seen them today," Doña Juana said, smiling hospitably. "Please come in. Your *menudo* won't be ready until tomorrow, but you have the fresh meat of my cow. My man is not here, but come in anyway."

Bill smiled at the invitation. Custom dictated that no man dismount and go into a house when he found a woman alone at a ranch, and Doña Juana was keeping an account. The captain jumped down off his horse and raged into the house. This set Pascual to laughing.

"That's right, giggle, *compadre*," Bill said crossly. "You haven't had your quota of fun today."

"*Compadrito*," Pascual said. "That monkey is making me happy. I hope he hears me and comes after us and quits bothering my mother."

The captain erupted from the house, ranting, and waving his pistol. He mounted his horse, wheeled the troops about, and led them to the trail Pascual and Bill had taken into the canyon.

"Ah, God is good," said Pascual.

The captain's high-headed palomino was a dancer, fine for parades and fiestas in town, but no horse for rock and mountains. The captain had chosen the palomino for his good looks. Cavalry regulations required that the mounts be only browns, sorrels, blacks, and bays—no off-colored horses.

The captain was anxious. The palomino was harried and nervous. The captain spurred his horse into the canyon, and the horse did not pick up his head at the bottom. The captain's weight speared the palomino's head into the bottom of the canyon, and he somersaulted off the horse, across a slab of smooth rock and out of sight. The soldiers bunched on the slab above the captain, while the sergeant dismounted and walked down to help him.

Pascual pulled the *tapojo* down over his mule's eyes, and dismounted. He tied his great, billowing *armas*—a cape of leather protection against the brush—high to her tail. He mounted, took a deep seat, and lifted the blindfold. He smiled at Bill. The mule trembled with nervous energy. Bill knew by looking at *La Divorciada* that she could kick his eyes out if he stayed behind her on his pokey mule. He moved La Loca ahead of Pascual.

La Divorciada knew she had been wronged while she was under the blindfold. She began to search for the nature of the insult. She was used to being insulted by Pascual. She knew her usual reaction to insult so well she was afraid of herself, but she loved mischief and was ready to do the evil that was expected of her. A muscle twitched in her eyelid at the same time her tail jerked with a nervous spasm. The stiff *armas* made a sound like writhing vipers behind her, and she turned and found them hanging on her most sensitive place, her tail.

Pascual howled, and spurred her so tufts of her hair flew in the breeze. *La Divorciada* sprang so high on her first jump, the *armas* popped and made an echo in the canyon. La Loca tucked her tail like a cowering dog. *La Divorciada* bawled her misery, wiped both sides of the canyon with the *armas,* and drove Bill and La Loca toward the soldiers. La Loca ran along, watching *La Divorciada* over her shoulder. The soldiers saw the wreck coming, and their horses began scrambling over one another to get out of the way. Bill and Pascual squalled and fired their pistols, and the mules stampeded into the mob.

"One side, one side, get over to one side," Bill shouted as *La Loca* plunged over a ledge above the soldiers. Horses were climbing over one another and slipping and falling on the slabs of rock. The captain was pinned under the palomino, and the troopers were trying to keep their horses from trampling him. Bill drove two horses over the top of the captain and set him to cursing. The captain fired his pistol and brought another horse down on himself. *La Loca* vaulted to clear the captain and two downed soldiers, and the captain looked Bill straight in the eye. He was hatless and his face was bleeding. His pistol hand was pinned under the horse he shot. A trooper was down on his back looking at Bill, and La Loca landed on his chest with both front feet, forcing a shout of agony from him.

Bill and Pascual hunted their way through the madness, left the tumult behind, and broke out of the canyon. On the meadow, *La Divorciada* passed *La Loca* like a racehorse. *La Loca* lost heart as the sight of her sister diminished toward the timber. She began to hump and balk under Bill's spurs.

A soldier recovered enough to climb out of the canyon

and begin firing his mauser at Bill. The noise put an end to *La Loca*. She planted her front feet, bowed her head, bawled, and quit with her mouth wide open.

"*Espérame, compadre. Espérame tantito.* Wait just a little for me, *compadre*," Bill shouted. He had been holding his breath. He let it go, laughing. He knew he would go muleback no more that day.

"*Lo siento, compadrito, pero espero Madre.* I feel for you, *compadre*, but I will not wait for even the mother," Pascual shouted, and he ran on into the timber.

Bill jumped off La Loca and started running across the meadow in his bullhide leggings and iron spurs. Two troopers came out of the canyon on horseback, ran him down, tied him with his own *reata*, and dragged him back into the canyon.

The troopers were still trying to peel their comrades off the rock. They glared at Bill. He had hoped for at least one smile or joke from the Mexicans. They unsaddled the palomino and let him up off their captain. The captain cursed and vomited. His fine palomino's front leg was broken below the knee. It whipped in front of him like a club when he tried to take a step. A trooper helped him to hop down the canyon and then shot him.

"*Lástima caballo.* What a waste of a good horse," said Bill to commiserate with the troopers and to see if they might have some compassion. The soldier nearest him struck him ineffectually on the chest with his open palms, pushing him into the Sergeant. The Sergeant, without seeming to consider any of the mechanics of the act, expertly broke Bill's nose with the butt of his quirt.

The soldiers dragged Bill out of the ravine, behind a horse. He came to his senses on Doña Juana's veranda. His jacket and chaps were hooked to his flesh with cactus thorns, and he had shed hide and hair on every foot of the trail from the bottom of the canyon.

Doña Juana made the Sergeant untie Bill so he could strip

and soak in a water trough to soften the cactus spines in his hide. She sat him naked on a cot beside the captain and picked the stickers out of him. The Sergeant decided Bill would tell him where Pascual had gone. Bill told him he did not know, and the Sergeant struck him playfully on the brow with the butt of his quirt. The Sergeant smiled and raised the quirt over Bill's head again. Bill lunged for the quirt, and the sergeant stepped back and struck him to his knees.

"Huh! Look at him," said the Sergeant, tracing the scar on Bill's back with the poppers on his quirt. "Somebody already shot him."

"*¡Canalla!*" Doña Juana cried. "Mobster, gangster. Hit me, why don't you? I'm a Yaqui and I'm at war with you. I'm also a woman who can't hit back. You're not at war with this man. He is not a Yaqui, a woman, or a child."

"I don't know how to hit women," said the Sergeant.

"Forget that I am a woman then. Hit me because I'm a Yaqui, but don't hit this man anymore."

"I respect you, señora, as I respect motherhood and womanhood. I love my own mother and the Virgin of Guadalupe." The Sergeant blessed himself piously for Doña Juana.

"You respect your mother, *Canalla*?"

"Yes, *señora*, but I don't want to be called *Canalla*. Please don't call me that. I'm a soldier."

"Then leave this young man alone and take your cowardly, southern, *guacho* face away from here. Leave women, children, and wounded men in peace. We have brave men in these mountains if you want someone to fight."

At that moment, some troopers brought a fresh horse for the captain. They helped him to his feet. His pistol was still in his hand and attached to a lanyard around his neck.

"*¡Ay, que dolor!* What pain!" the captain said, groaning and holding the pistol over his heart. He combed his hair with his left hand and did not put the pistol down. He had not holstered it since he had drawn it in the canyon. Bill saw that the captain was only suffering from *susto*—the shock of fright—and a few dashing bruises.

Bill dressed, and the Sergeant pushed him out the door and off the veranda. Bill's wounds were hot and seeping blood, but they no longer worried him. The cactus thorns did not hurt, either. They only pestered him.

The soldiers mounted and started away, leading Bill on foot. As soon as he was out of sight of Doña Juana, the Sergeant halted the troop and ordered two men to fall back to Bill. Another turn in the trail and Bill would have run for the canyon again. One of the troopers who fell back was carrying a heavy oxen yoke across his saddle. The Sergeant's grin stretched the welts across his scarred face. Bill knew the Yaquis called him The Embroidered One. All of a sudden the man's face struck him funny and he laughed. He knew the *guachos* intended to walk him to death and he did not care. He was no longer tired. He wanted a chance to fight and if he could not fight, he could laugh at them.

"Now, Yankee ox," the Sergeant said in a good humor; because he felt he had plenty of reasons for punishing Bill. "Oxen must learn to endure their thumps and prodding, and you are overdue for yours. You'll carry your yoke in the furrow until you learn to stay in line."

The soldiers lifted the thick, hardwood yoke to Bill's neck and tied his arms over the top. They passed the rope through rings on each end of the yoke and rode away, pulling the yoke at a generous pace.

The Sergeant rode behind Bill and poked him on the tailbone with a sharp stick when he faltered. He liked to prod a certain spot on the end of Bill's tailbone. He encouraged progress best when he poked Bill there.

"*Arre, arre, mi buey.* Drive on, my ox," the sergeant chanted. "This is the way we soldiers till the soil for a new Mexico." The point of the stick invariably found the same nerve on Bill's tail until the spot was so sore it knew when the stick was coming and flinched when the stick was still a yard away.

With the weight of his arms tied over the yoke, Bill could not walk far without stumbling. Each time he fell, the yoke drove his face into the trail. The troopers who were leading him jerked alternately at each end of the yoke to make it more alive on his shoulders. Bill would have had to be dead ten days to be insensitive to the point of the sergeant's stick.

Near a red cliff in the Pass of Canelas, he heard a shot, and the captain's horse fell dead, pinning the captain to the ground again and blocking the trail. Pascual called out and politely asked the captain to surrender his troops.

"We are seven rifles here, captain," Pascual called. "We'll kill you in three volleys and you'll never be out of our sights. Surrender."

The sergeant prodded Bill forward, confident he could bargain with Pascual. Bill let himself fall near the captain and stayed down.

"Do you see this refuse I've been driving ahead of me, Matus?" the sergeant shouted. "Show yourself like a man and tell me what to do with it. It is your garbage, is it not?" He poked Bill again. Bill knew the Sergeant must have been an expert at driving oxen. He never missed the nerve he had made sore.

The captain was shrieking orders to his soldiers. No one had moved to help him.

"*El Bordado,* ask your leader to please shut up so you can hear me," Pascual shouted. "He's making me tired. I want to know how my *Yanqui compadre* works under the *yoke.*" Pascual was laughing. "Is he good enough to plow his *quota?* What sort of partner would he be in a *yunta,* a team of oxen."

The Sergeant found a new nerve with the stick, a live one that caused Bill to squeak and pump his legs. "A lame one, don't you see?" the sergeant shouted. "He limps and balks, stumbles and kicks. He's probably useless. I think I'll just shoot him now and stop his suffering." He raised his pistol, in a good humor, joking.

Bill heard a bullet crack the Sergeant's skull, and the Sergeant's weight drilled the butt of the prod stick between Bill's sore shoulders. Then the sound of Pascual's rifle echoed against the red cliff. Bill fainted and nearly suffocated under the Sergeant.

The Captain opened his mouth wide and bellowed, *"We surrender, please, please, please. We surrender. What do you want? We'll give it to you!"*

"That's all right," Pascual answered. "Just give me back that *jodido,* that poor, befouled, lame, American ox."

The soldiers quickly untied Bill, lifted the yoke, and helped him to his feet. Pascual ordered the soldiers to picket the horses and pile all their packs, weapons, and boots by the trail. He scolded them, called them foolish Mexicans, and ordered them to leave the Sierra without stopping to eat or sleep.

When the soldiers were gone, Pascual showed himself by the trail. Six of his neighbors came out to pack the horses with the weapons, boots, and packs. Bill could not speak when Pascual came and embraced him.

"Don't bawl, now, like a calf," Pascual said, looking into Bill's face. He laughed and slapped Bill's shoulders.

"If I bawl it will be from pure *coráje,*" Bill said. He *was* on the verge of bawling. "Pure rage." He looked around and walked to El Bordado's body. He put his toe under the carcass and rolled it over to look at the face. The bullet had done awful things to his eyes.

"Look at *you,* you son of a bitch," Bill said.

Pascual laughed. Then he said:

> *"Compadrito Beel en mula baya,*
> *Vale mas que no vaya.*
> *Compadre* Bill as a rule,
> Should not ride the dun mule."

CHAPTER 5

In Mexico, a master horseman and trainer is called a caballerango. *From this word, American cowboys took the* rango *and made it* wrangler.

People who think they are wranglers, but do not know their business, say a horse's performance must be wrested and wrangled from him. The good a horse can do them only provokes their greed and sloth, never their generosity.

A true caballerango *believes that a horse is convinced of his own place in creation and does not need to beg man for his existence. As a creature of God, a horse is at least forty million years older than man, and he never had to trample, pollute, or kill to arrive at his present state.*

AT La Escondida, a troop of *La Cordada* almost surprised Lindano in his sleep. He hurried off his pallet and hid Copper in the brush just as the troop passed by. He hid in a willow thicket by a stream and ate the last of the jerky he had brought from the garrison. He was not surprised that he had awakened just in time to escape capture by *La Cordada:* he was lucky at escaping his enemies. His friendship with the Devil spared him more often than not.

Lindano stayed and spied on the ranch. He saw that Cabezón hid Placido, Mary, and Steeldust from La Cordada, too. The troops of La Cordada rested, feasted on Cabezón's beef for a day and a night, and then headed back to the north. La Cordada was made up of ranchers and *vaqueros* from northern Sonora. They did not like to fight in the south where the *monte,* the brush, was thick. They traveled as far south as Alamos, but only for meetings. They stayed on the trails when they were in the south. They did not hunt or chase the southern *amarradores,* the cattle thieves who went afoot and maneuvered like ocelots in the brush. The *amarradores* fought close, from ambush, with *reatas* and machetes. The men of La Cordada would not fight unless they could fight on horseback, so they did not bother with thieves who skulked on foot in the brush.

After La Cordada had gone, Placido and Mary came out of the house and saddled Steeldust. Cabezón gave Placido a young mare he had raised and a saddle. She was out of a Mexican mare and by a Shetland stud he had brought from the States. He was developing a short, tough breed of cowhorse for his *vaqueros* to ride in the brush.

Cabezón and his *vaqueros* took Placido and Mary with them to a pasture where they gathered a hundred fat bulls and oxen and started driving them toward the coast. Lindano followed the drive to the port of Lobos where Cabezón sold the beef to a fishing fleet. Placido and Mary left Cabezón at Lobos and headed south.

Lindano was content. The children were going exactly the way he wanted them to go. South on the coast lay his secret place. He loved the place. Last year he had taken some time off there with a woman of the same stamp as Margara. The poor woman had not enjoyed the outing as much as he. His white beach was on the edge of millions of acres of brush, where only the jaguars and ocelots and Mayo Indians felt at home. No one ever bothered Lindano there, or saw what he did.

It seemed to Lindano that every new development in the kidnapping of Mary proved to him that he was doing right. He had been hoping Cabezón would want to be rid of Mary and Placido. Cabezón was a businessman, and he certainly did not want to make enemies by protecting Placido. He would be given much credit by the Yaquis for saving Placido from Echeverria, anyway. All the children had to do was reach the Mayo River and the whole Mayon nation would protect them. Cruz, Placido's mother, was Mayo. The Mayos were not at war with the government anymore. *La Cordada* did not enter the Mayo brush for any reason.

Lindano hoped Placido would find his mother on the Mayo. When he mothered up, he would stay in one place awhile. Before long, Pascual would join them, and then Lindano would get the cavalry to imprison the whole family. He would have Mary to himself once again. The cavalry would pay him his bounty for the Matus family, and after he was through with Mary, he would sell her back to R.E. Bradford. Lindano was satisfied. His patience and good business practices were resolving themselves logically, as usual. This only proved that when a man was businesslike in his manner, he soon attained success. No logical person could blame him for capitalizing on a situation he had created; it was such good business.

Placido and Mary rode down a wide trail along the Mayo River. The river was overgrown with Alamo trees. The river shade was cool. Mary kept looking at the clear water. All her life she had wanted to live by quiet, shady water and know all day that it was flowing by. They rode under a big Guayava tree, and a flock of parrots flew crankily out of the top, flew high, and complained until it was out of sight.

Cruz was singing loudly and happily when Placido and Mary rode into her clearing. She was making tortillas and enjoying a breeze under her *ramada*. She stopped singing and laughed when she recognized Placido. Four corn *gordas* were braising on a piece of tin over Cruz's fire. Mary smelled the aroma of the corn dough, and her mouth watered. Placido had not told her where they were, but Mary hoped this was their destination. Cruz rinsed her hands in a wooden bowl and kept smiling at Placido. She did not seem to notice Mary and Steeldust.

"Hello, son," Cruz said. "What could have brought you back without your father?"

"This person brings me here, Mother," Placido said. He and Mary dismounted, and he led her up to stand in front of Cruz. Cruz took Mary's face in her cool hands, looked at her eyes, brushed mud from her face, and smoothed her hair.

"¡Ay! Qué muchacha—and those eyes!" said Cruz, as though Mary needed scolding. She wet a cloth, sat Mary down, and washed her face. "Do you know, son, when you rode up I was thinking of the time we raised flowers here with your father. We thrived on this ground, and no one bothered us. Imagine, I was thinking of you and your father, and singing songs, and here you are. Where is your father?"

Mary looked at Cruz and saw a girl who could be her own age. Her brown skin was smooth and clear, her teeth white and square. Perspiration beaded the bridge of her nose and upper lip and splashed the hair at the temples. She was of ancient Mayo stock that drank musso tea daily for a tonic and lived to be a hundred and twenty years old.

Mary sat with a cup of coffee in the quiet breeze and listened to Cruz. Mary always spoke her Spanish softly so her accent would not call attention to her. To listen more and speak less was a new way for Mary to be. She liked it. She answered Cruz's questions about her mother's methods of growing flowers. She promised to bring Cruz flower seed the next time she visited. Cruz did not mention that she knew Mary had been running for her life.

In the days Cruz had grown her flowers, the Mayos had been fighting with the Yaquis against the government. Pascual had been wounded in a fight at Pueblo Viejo on the Rio Mayo. He had brought Cruz and Placido to this camp called Chihuahuita to recuperate and farm a crop of alfalfa. One of Placido's sisters was born during that time. While he was healing, Pascual stayed to cut the alfalfa for his cows. He milked them, and Cruz made cheese while they raised the calves. The calves were yearlings when Pascual butchered them. He traded the cows for mules, turned his mares loose in the Alameda, and went back to the fighting on the Yaqui River.

Mary realized she had been wrong believing Pascual was a murdering savage. She could imagine him at peace in Chihuahuita. She could see him stepping inside a herd to see what it needed and scattering feed for it.

Placido took a scythe and went away to cut grass for Steeldust and his mare. When he returned, he was taking quick steps under a big bundle of green feed and carrying a sack of dried corn. He dropped the corn at Mary's feet so she could rub the kernels off the cobs for the horses. She already knew how to do that.

Mary did not lose one minute finding peace at Chihuahuita. She felt at home the minute she met Cruz, even though she was far from any place a Bradford would ordinarily light. Now, she could sit under a *ramada* with a simple supper and watch parrots fly, listen to the Patagonia pigeons sing, and watch the pichiquila tree ducks fly home.

Mary appreciated Cruz's cleanliness and the way she kept cleaning—even though she was barefoot on a dirt floor, her children mostly naked. The two little girls' bellies swelled over their cotton bloomers. The boy's bare, dusty butt was tough as leather from sitting on the ground at play.

Cruz served her meals on tortillas. She and her children slept together on a *petate,* a straw mat she spread on the ground and rolled up with her bedding in the daytime. Mary did not ask the classic American visitor's question, "How do people live like this?" She lived there, too.

Steeldust and Placido's mare began to thrive. One side of their corral bordered Cruz's kitchen and Steeldust watched Cruz and Mary all day as they worked. He became a *tortillero,* begging Cruz for tortillas with soulful looks, his head over the fence by the fire. He relished tortillas. The flies did not bother his eyes when he kept his head in the kitchen near the fire.

In the mornings, the children went with Mary to exercise Steeldust. Mary did not want him to get fat and soft. She might have to leave in a hurry. She wanted to learn the trails around Chihuahuita and know her way out through the brush. Placido drew the outline of Steeldust's hooves on paper, made new shoes at the forge in Chihuahuita, and shod him. Mary and the children kept him brushed and rubbed, his mane and tail combed. The horse filled out and began to shine again.

A week after Mary and Steeldust came to the Mayo, a delegation from Chihuahuita headed by a big Mayo *Cacique*, a chief, named Ursulo, came to talk. Mary hid in the dark sleeping room behind straw walls in a corner of the *ramada*. One of the men who accompanied Ursulo was Marco, the state appointed *Comisario*, a commissioner of the state law of the region. The men greeted Cruz politely and then stood by and waited for Placido to talk to them. They did not look at the horses, nor at Cruz, nor inside her *ramada*. Cruz poured coffee for them, and Placido carried it to them and held the sugar bowl while they sweetened it. Then, Ursulo squatted with the delegation in the shade of a *jito* tree and drank the coffee. When they finished, they set the cups on the ground.

"So this is the horse we hear about on the radio," Ursulo said. "Who would have thought a kinsman of mine would bring such a horse to our region?"

"What kinsman of yours?" Placido asked.

"You and your mother are our kin, are you not?"

"Yes, but I did not bring the horse. I did not come alone from the north. The horse was ridden here by his owner."

"Is it true the horse was stolen by Lindano and was used to carry a girl he kidnapped?"

"That is true."

"You have the horse, but who owns him?"

"Someone else."

"Ah, is the owner in the United States?"

"The owner is here with the horse."

"The owner must be wealthy to own such a horse. We who give the horse a peaceful place to stay are poor. Since you are protecting the property of this horse owner, he'll probably make you wealthy like himself. You are also the son of a wealthy Yaqui horse owner, Pascual Matus. We wonder what you want to pay for the safety of the stallion and his owner."

"I also have been wondering how to pay you. I know my mother belongs here, because she is Mayan. I guess I must also have rights here because of her. I'm not sure how you should be paid for the horse and his owner. My father will have to be the one to decide, when he arrives, if he finds the horse and the owner have been kept safe."

"We guarantee your safety, the horse's, and the owner's. We will not talk about rights. Here, you are all at home. The payment is up to you, young man."

"I have little money. I don't know how to satisfy you unless you tell me what payment you will accept."

"When will Matus be here?"

"Soon."

"You were correct in coming here. Use our pasture for your horses. Come to our stores for anything you need, as always. However, if you want to pay us, you can do it before Pascual comes. You have the resources yourself."

Ursulo and his delegation moved to the corral and leaned against it to watch Steeldust eat, finally availing themselves of their privilege of an open appraisal of the horse.

"Ah," Ursulo said.

"Look, you can see every nerve, muscle, and sinew under that clear coat," said Marco. "*That* is a horse."

"So this is the *Estíldos*," said Ursulo. "I thought I knew what a horse looked like, until now. What does this mean, *Estíldos*? Two styles, like *dosestilos*?" Ursulo laughed at himself softly, knowing he was wrong, admitting he was ignorant.

"My father told me it means *polvo de acero* in English."

"Ah, he's named, perhaps, for his temper, or his strength," said Marco. "He looks more like the dust of gold. What fine ardor must have shaped him. What hot blood he brings down from his fathers. Those *huevos,* those eggs, of his could change the look of every horse in this poor country."

"He can't be mounting our mares. He might have to run with his owner at any moment."

"We'll respect him, then," Ursulo said. "But maybe someday he could leave us a colt, one colt at least." Ursulo subsided a moment, making sure Placido knew he was disappointed. "If you won't allow him to service our mares, what else can he do besides bring the cavalry down on us?"

"He can do anything better than any other horse alive."

"Ah, can he pull a plow? Tread the millstone?"

"Steeldust was not bred to be worked."

"For herding goats, then?"

"Not for herding goats, either. I know he's a great cow horse, though."

"But we've only been able to see how he eats. He's not very special in the way he eats, and I bet he does not look so elegant and shiny when he's been hungry awhile."

"If we had cattle, would he move them for us as elegantly as he removes his corn?" Marco asked, smiling.

"Yes," Placido said.

"We do not require that our cows be moved with elegance, since we have no cows."

"How can he pay for his keep while he's here?" Ursulo asked. "If he can't breed our mares, herd our goats, gather our cattle, or plow our fields, can we pack him like a burro to bring in wood? He looks big enough to carry the loads of three burros. The way he eats, if he can't do it now, he'll be able to do it next week. How long will he be eating like this?"

"Not the load of one burro, nor of three. Steeldust is not a packhorse."

"Then, he can only stand and eat while he is here?"

"He can buck if you try to ride him."

"Bucking would be of no service to us. Can he run?"

"No horse in this region has ever been bred, or ever been dropped on his head at birth with sufficient force, as my father says, to make him fast enough to stay in sight of this horse's heels in a race. Steeldust brings the speed of a horse to the Mayo people for the first time in their history."

"Ah, then, he might be worth the risk we're taking to keep him here. You think he can run? Allow us to see him run, then."

"I suppose we could pretend to race. If you have a horse to compare to him and if seeing him run will convince you he's worth your protection, I'll let him run four hundred *varas* for you."

"You know our horse, *Pluma Roja,* the great sorrel of *pura sangre,* the thoroughbred horse General Cazares gave us? Your Steeldust might be a match for him, but he's never been outrun."

"You don't understand this horse's kind of speed. I'm talking about speed a *guerrero,* a warrior, needs when he has to disappear in the brush in the blink of an eye. Not a long lope that might run down a coyote in half a day. Not the pace a hare uses to go from the Mayo to the Yaqui. I'm talking about the speed of lightning that stuns, not the lighting of a match that reveals a figure in the dark."

"Then, let us be stunned. It will be our privilege."

"Then, someday you might take Pluma Roja to a place where Steeldust is being exercised. Steeldust's owner might want to let him run to expand his lungs. *Pluma Roja's caballerango* might trot him out to the same place. If both horses are of the same spirit, they might run at the same time."

"In three weeks at the *brecha* in the *alameda* of Chihuahuita?"

"Let's run in three days."

"Fine, what do you wager?"

"I only want to be able to keep the horse on the Mayo in peace."

"That would happen even without a race. What prize do you want if you win?"

"I guess he has to win his peace, just the same as everyone else does. I wouldn't want you to complain that Steeldust may have been able to perform great deeds, but you saw him do none."

"We accept. We'll give him feed and care for his lifetime and we'll admire him. What do you have to lose, though?"

"If Steeldust does not run the greatest four hundred *varas* you've ever seen, I'll surrender to the government as your captive. You can have money and prestige for my ears. If my ears are not acceptable, I'll wager an *alazán,* the one given me by my father for the purpose of paying my way where money is required. He took this coin from an enemy after he choked him in a tree."

"Ah, a precious coin," Ursulo said. "Or a precious life. There could be no higher wager. Gold has the value of a life, nowadays. Coin often protects a life. I might someday have to spend your life if I won it in this race. We never know what we have to spend to survive in a war with the Yoris. We'll wager an *alazán* with you and we'll have our horse at the *brecha,* the cleared stretch in the *alameda* of Chihuahuita, before sunrise in three days."

"We'll run our horse the moment the lower rim of the sun clears the *cerro,* or the starter shouts, '*Santiago,*' " said Placido.

"*Pluma Roja* will be there and Marco will judge the start."

For the next two days Mary played with Cruz's children and Steeldust under the big trees along the river. The children swam with Steeldust in deep water, mounting him and sliding him down the bank into the river. He always swam in a circle once, looking for a place to climb out, then paddled downstream with the current. The children trailed along, holding his mane and tail until his feet touched the ground and he walked out. After the swim, they stood him in a patch of sun, wiped the water off him, and caressed him while he dozed.

Steeldust was careful of the children and he tolerated their games. At night, he slept close inside the sound of their breathing. He depended on them for his feed, his shelter, his exercise, and his diversion. Their attention did not make him shabby, weary, or plodding. Their pursuits were happy and helped him prosper. He never balked or refused them. He never shied and jumped aside from real, invented, or imagined dangers so he could get away from them. He was not afraid of a snake or a black stump when he carried Mary and the children. He did not mind if the children rode him when Mary was not around. If a child fell off him, he stopped and waited and endured the tugs and pinches of gripping fingers and toes until the child remounted. He tolerated the giggling and squirming in the same mood he endured the weeping and the small, angry blows when a child blamed him for injuries. He never ran away and left them. He watched for them if they went off and left him.

The afternoon before the race, Placido and Mary rode out to find Pascual's band of mares. The mares had been running wild for two years. They had escaped many attempts by the *amarradores* to corral them. Placido thought he and Mary should try to pen them. The *amarradores* had gone after them on foot and let them get away so many times they would be hard to drive out of the brush. Placido had one great advantage. He had a stud horse and the mares did not.

Placido was his father's son, and he could not resist bringing Steeldust's speed, power, and good humor to the mares. He was not a fool to bring the stud four hundred miles through every kind of trouble a man could find and not think of taking the horse's seed for his father's mares.

Placido found the mares with several mule colts by their sides. When they first saw the riders, they trotted away. They knew they could get away. Then they smelled the stud, and it addled them so they could not get away. They pranced and lifted their tails and trailed each other in a wide arc that kept bending back toward Steeldust. They sashayed and postured for Steeldust, and he began to realize he was a stud. He was sure he was ready to give the females anything they wanted, just as soon as he found out what it was.

The mares followed him because they wanted to stay with him. Mary rode ahead of them, Placido rode behind them, and Steeldust led them in. Placido shut them inside his father's field by his mother's *ramada*.

That night, the din of mares neighing, calling, crying, and squealing was so great that everyone in the region knew Steeldust had brought romance to the Matus mares. The Mayos decided that Pascual must also be on his way back. Horse business always began when Matus was close.

On the morning of the race, Placido still had not told Mary that Steeldust was pledged to run. He awakened her early and told her to mount her horse bareback. He mounted his mare and led Mary out through the brush. She followed Placido obediently in pitch darkness.

At dawn they broke into a big clearing, and Mary saw a crowd of silent Mayos waiting by a fire. Straight *saguaro* stakes a yard long had been driven into the ground at one-yard intervals down a straightaway. Mary kept her head down and listened to find out what she was doing there. Placido rode to the men and spoke to them in Mayo. Mary rode around the clearing and kept her eyes on Steeldust's ears.

Then Placido came to her and wrapped a thick length of coarse linen over her knees and tied it around Steeldust's girth, tightening her legs against Steeldust's barrel. The cloth held her perched and kneeling on his broad back, her knees thrust through the cloth, her feet trailing.

"You're riding your horse in a race," Placido said.

"¿*Como*? How's that? A race? When?"

"Now. Right now."

"¿*Como*?"

"Just listen. You have to make this horse run, now. The other horse will be here in a minute. I'll show you where to line up. Keep your horse behind the starting line. The race will begin when the starter shouts the word *Santiago,* or when the bottom rim of the sun rises clear of the mountain. Watch the rhythm of the breath of the starter and you'll know when to go. Run your horse on your side of the *varas,* the stakes that are lined down the track. Watch the stakes and stay close to them. They are there to keep the horses apart. Do not watch the men at the finish line. They will crowd closer and closer toward the stakes as your horse nears the finish. They'll leave you only the width of your horse to cross the finish. If your horse is frightened by the crowd, he'll never cross the line, and we'll lose."

"What if I run over one of them?"

"If you do, I hope Steeldust recovers enough to win. If you hit somebody, you won't just trample one, you'll probably trample twenty. They'll all surge together toward the track at the finish. I'll be sitting on my horse in your path beyond the finish. Run to me. Don't pull up until you reach me."

"Why do they press the finish line? Is that part of the contest?"

"They're not supposed to get in your way, but if you don't cross the finish line first, you don't win."

"Then I'm guaranteed they'll let Steeldust cross the finish line?"

"Ah, they'll move in to see the finish better and that will be involuntary. They can't help it. They'll also crowd in to frighten your horse so he'll refuse at the line."

"You tell them I give them fair warning—If they get in the way, my Steeldust will have to flatten them."

"Don't worry about them. They want us to lose the race, but they don't want to die."

Just then Mayo horsemen rode into the clearing, escorting *Pluma Roja* and his rider. The *caballerango* and jockey was an old man, half Mary's size. He was burned black by the sun. The Mayos called him *Sombra*, Shadow.

Steeldust was much wider than *Pluma Roja*, but the Mayo horse was taller. He showed hunter blood in his great head and big bones. He was stepping high and showing a fierce eye to the world. A red plume bobbed on the headstall between his ears.

"Matus, if you wish, we'll furnish you a good jockey," said Ursulo. "You need one who is light and wiry, and has strong hands."

"Our horse will be the first to cross the finish line and our jockey will be with the horse," Placido said.

"Fine, but we want to know something. Is your horse here to run a race, or cause an earthquake? He's too wide to run an ordinary race, isn't he? Wouldn't he run better sideways? His rider is too large to be a jockey."

Mary glanced quickly at the Mayos. She was a small girl, but she could see she outweighed *Sombra* by at least twenty pounds. None of the Mayos were looking at her. A small group of Mexicans standing apart from the Mayos were all staring at her.

"At least let us furnish you with a strong man to ride your horse for the contest, not a big, soft child," Ursulo said. "A slim man with wise hands will make your horse show his speed. Anyone with eyes as clear as your jockey's is too innocent for this contest. Your rider's hands are too slim, his back too weak, to take charge of so big a horse. How will he help the horse? Is he a sorcerer with eyes like that? He will have to be a sorcerer to win this race. No horse would run for a jockey with blue eyes. Tell him not to look at *Pluma*

Roja. Our horse has never been seen by blue eyes and this is not the day to initiate him. I know, you are using this jockey so we'll bet more money. All right, we'll bet another *alazán.*"

Placido laughed softly. "So, it turns out you have money. No one in the world would know it unless they ran you a horse race. I have one more *alazán* to bet, but no more. I don't want your money."

The Mayos knew Mary was an American girl, but they would not show it. They kept their eyes on Steeldust when they looked her way. They spoke Spanish when they wanted to make sure she understood, however. Mary kept her eyes to herself. She wanted to ask questions about this horse race, but she did not want to call attention to herself. The Mayos gave her plenty of room. The men she had encountered on the trails had looked straight ahead as they passed her and then hurried quickly on, before Mary could make a sign to them. The Mayos were making such an effort to make her feel safe that they even hid themselves from her.

Mary began loping Steeldust on the track to warm him. She held him in a straight line past the finish and then stopped him in line before she turned back, as she had seen her father's jockeys do. She wanted Steeldust to know he had to run straight and stay on the track as though he were on rails.

Near the time for the start, Placido caught up and rode with Mary. "You'll run at the sound of the word, *Santiago,*" he said. "However, the starter will be trying to let you go anytime after the top of the sun shows over the hill. He will start the race only if all four of Steeldust's feet and all four of *Pluma Roja's* feet are standing still on the line at the same time. If all eight feet never stand on the ground at the same time, he'll start you when the bottom of the sun clears the mountain.

"Don't watch the other jockey, or the other horse. Stand your horse behind the line and watch the breath of the starter. He has to take a deep breath to shout the word."

Mary nodded as though she understood. She had seen a hundred quarter-horse races started lap and tap from a run. To go from a standing start seemed a lot easier. Steeldust would stand still. Her only problem might be to keep him awake for the race. She had never jockeyed a race, but she was not going to admit it to Placido. Girls never got to do this, anywhere. She thought she knew how to ride to win, but she was grateful that Placido was coaching her. He was showing her great respect, so she would never let him know she did not know what she was doing. Anyway, she knew Steeldust could outrun this gargoyle-headed dink farther than *"Sombra"* could throw a rock.

"Remember, a short race like this is decided by the start. If you sleep on the starting line, you'll never catch Pluma Roja. This race will be won before your horse draws a deep breath."

"Yes, yes, let's go," said Mary. "Line my horse up and let the whole tribe try to keep him off the finish line. Steeldust will lay them down and leave them for dead."

"All right, it's time. Go to the starting line."

Mary's heart sprang to the race. She took hold of Steeldust as Marco motioned for her horse to stand in front of him. Steeldust came alive when he walked by *Pluma Roja*. The muscles along his back swelled and squeezed Mary's legs against the cloth. He knew it was time for him to run for his life. He did not care if he ran his adversary to death. He felt he would expire if he was outrun, or if he was not allowed to run. Mary concentrated on keeping him in bounds so he would not waste the breath he was building for the race. She coached herself with advice she had heard Bill give her father's jockeys. Ride in one place on a horse's back and sit still. Don't shift on him. Whip close to his side and don't wave. Don't kick the air out of him every jump. Don't kick him at all. Take hold of him, yell in his ear, and show him his demons, don't just sit up there for the ride. Keep him straight on the track and steady his head. Lose his head, and you lose the race, maybe the horse's life, and your own life too. Say a Hail Mary, give your soul to God, your fanny to the horse, and let the sonofabitch run.

Marco used a hardwood baton to direct the horses to the starting line. He wanted them both to stand still for just an instant with all their feet on the ground, so he could see a fair start. He gave instructions in Mayo under his breath. Mary understood him by watching the baton. The sun was burning over the Sierra. Mary rode Steeldust to the line. The horse was willing to keep the law and stand still at the line. Pluma Roja kept coming to the line and dancing so he would not have to pause there. He wanted to hit the line on the go. Marco kept directing *Sombra* to take his horse back and come to the line again. Steeldust was standing still, looking down his side of the track wistfully, as though he wished he could have a running start the same as any other exuberant horse. He had never been in a horse race in his life, but he knew he was in one now.

By asking him to stand still, Mary wanted noble behavior that did not come easy for a horse. But Steeldust knew how to behave and he intended to win. *"Tenía mucha ley,"* as the Mexicans say. He was a lawful horse. Horses knew horse races long before man knew horses. Man could never have invented horse races. He could not have imagined what a horse brought to a race until he saw horses racing.

Pluma Roja had run many races, and had left every opponent dead in his dust. He did not like stopping and standing and pausing before he ran. He knew if he kept dancing at the line, he would wear the starter's patience until he was allowed to go. He was confident he would have his way with men and horses as usual that day. He never let the starter see all four of his feet touch down at once. He used the hearts and eyes in his feet and always held one foot a fraction above the ground, sensitive to Marco's stare. When he stamped it down, another foot was already rising off the ground for Marco to see. Marco drew the breath to start the race four times, but each time let it out without a sound, because *Pluma Roja* would not rest that last foot upon the ground. *Sombra* kept taking him away and bringing him back.

Then, the bottom of the sun cleared the top of the Sierra Madre, and it was time to go. Marco did not shout the word. Mary became confused. She looked at *Sombra* for a sign they were still trying to start the race. *Pluma Roja* came to the line and was gone.

"*¡Santiago!*" shouted Marco at the top of his voice.

"*¡Se vinieron!*" shouted the Mayos. "They have come!"

Mary looked at Marco and then turned Steeldust loose. Down the track, in a big hurry, as far away as she could throw a rock, *Pluma Roja* was showing Mary the bottoms of his hooves and kicking dirt in her face. Then, with both hands tangled in Steeldust's mane, Mary began singing and laughing in his ear, because with his first three jumps she could see he would eat *Pluma Roja* alive in this horse race. Steeldust smoothly turned loose all his studhorse muscle and nerve—everything that had ever held him back—and no human being alive could have held him until the race was run.

Halfway down the track, Steeldust passed *Pluma Roja* as though his plume was stanchioned on the two-hundreth *vara*. *Pluma Roja* and *Sombra* were watching behind them to see if the other horse in the race might come along. They were still looking for another horse when Steeldust went by. The looks on their faces said the thing that passed them could not be a horse. Steeldust must have looked like a freight train to the Mayos at the finish line. From the halfway mark he came at them all alone. They did not crowd forward to judge which horse finished first. They backed out of Steeldust's way as he finished ten lengths ahead of *Pluma Roja*. *Pluma Roja* was outrun so badly he looked lame and disjointed when he came along to finish the race.

Mary began jockeying to bring Steeldust back to the ground. The horse's body began to shamble and quiver and fall in jolts on his front legs; His momentum kept coursing through him, trying to lift him in flight again while his flesh stayed behind. He regained his grace when the momentum coursed out of his body, but for those few moments at the end of the race, Mary had to stay with him to help him keep his feet as the flight left his carcass. That was the only part of the race where Mary had to do a jockey's work and bring the horse back under her control, bring him back to the pace of his flesh and blood.

Placido had been keeping pace with Steeldust on his mare. Steeldust quieted, and Mary rode back by the Mayos; when she glanced at them they were all smiling at her as if their horse had won the race.

"Now we've seen a horse *and* a jockey," Ursulo said.

"Nevertheless, your horse beat us at the start," Placido said. "Smart horse."

"Too bad the winners are not declared for the way they start. You had more horse. I wonder, however, could Steeldust run so well without a child with transparent eyes to direct him? With *Pluma Roja's* knowledge and such a rider to guide him, we might have done better."

"Forget it," Marco said. "Both Steeldust and his jockey were asleep at the starting line. They were not impatient at the start because they never doubted the outcome. A horse doesn't need to be a quick starter when he can run like that."

"*Pluma Roja* wanted to win, didn't he?" Ursulo asked. "He did his best, did he not?"

"To his disgrace, he won a five length head start, probably more," Marco said. "He was not surprised when Steeldust passed him, because he did not know that was a horse he saw go by. He did not know other horses could run that fast."

Mary was smiling at the Mayas, enjoying their admiration. The Mexicans kept their eyes cast down while they collected money they had won from the Mayas. They had bet on Steeldust. She watched the five Mexicans to see if one would show his face to her. Finally, one turned to face her. In that face she saw no happiness, no honest enjoyment, no admiration for the horse and rider who had just won him money. She saw mean old greed pinched in a face with whiskers on it. That Mexican was Lindano. Then the other four Mexicans looked at her with that same look. She turned to see if Placido knew the Mexicans.

"Those are *Los Amarradores*," said Placido. "Cattle and horse thieves. And look who is with them."

"I already saw him. What can he do? I'm horseback and he's on foot."

"Keep walking. When we get to the end of the track where no one can call us back, we'll just keep going."

"*¡Ai, mamacita!*" Lindano said, calling to Mary. "What fine *corvas*, hams, you have for gripping a stallion's bare back."

"Keep going, María," Placido said.

"Don't worry about me. Don't let them anger you."

Mary looked back. Lindano was smirking, but the Mayas had turned silently toward him and their disapproval had shut his mouth for a moment.

"Why do you keep looking back, María?" Placido asked. "Let's go, now. Don't look back and don't listen to them."

Another Mexican called after Mary. "For a mount, it would be hard to choose between the horse and the woman."

"They're cowards," Placido said. "Don't worry about them. They can't hurt you. The Mayas would nick and dull their machetes on their heads before they would let them hurt you."

Mary rode into the brush and let Steeldust lope toward Cruz's *ramada*. She looked back at Placido and saw he was embarrassed he had not done battle with Lindano. Instead of fighting, he was riding away from his enemy on a mare and following a girl who was riding the big stud. His pride was smarting.

"They're the cowards," Placido said when they stopped.

"Of course they are, Placido," Mary said. "Forget them."

"Those Mexicans are allowed to hide here because their women are Mayo. They live by catching Don Tomás Siqueros's yearling calves at night while the cattle lie on their bedground. That's all they're good for."

"I only worry Lindano will get his hands on Steeldust again."

"The Mayos will cut off his hands if he touches you or the horse. Steeldust has given them the example of a horse they'll remember the rest of their lives.

Lindano left the Mexicans at the *alameda* and followed Mary and Placido. He left Copper in a thicket and crossed the river on foot. He hid on his belly in a mesquite thicket close to Cruz's *ramada*. He watched Cruz, Mary, and Placido feeding horses, carrying wood, and cooking supper, as a stockman watches his livestock in its browsing. He kept an eye on the food his livestock ate and the shade it enjoyed. He wanted the stock to prosper.

Lindano never considered that his work might be wicked. Mary, the college girl, was valueless except for the pleasure she could give a man and the money her parents would pay to get her back. A man had to make a living. An audacious and ambitious man would be a fool to pass up the opportunity to create his own commodity, his own market, and his own sales conditions in a business.

In the end, to Lindano, all humans lived and died for money and the pleasure it bought them. All a man had to do to be a success among humans was make a lot of money. Lindano considered himself no worse than any other businessman as far as being wicked was concerned.

Money would be the final blessing on the entire kidnapping affair. R.E. would be able to say he gave every dollar of cash he could rake up to get his daughter back. The worthless girl would be able to brag that her father gave everything he owned for her recovery. Lindano would enjoy spending the money and keeping the horse. Everyone would know how good a businessman he was.

The wicked sins Lindano did would be the secret part of the affair that would heal and be forgotten. The ransom money would be replenished by the Bradford land and livestock; when the money hurts subsided, all the other hurts would fade. Only the girl would remember the ordeal, and she had the rest of her life to spend forgetting. Lindano would have the money to buy back God by doing fine deeds for various poor souls. Someday he would be the patron of so many that his enemies would have no voice at all.

At dark, Lindano backed out of the thicket and headed for Pueblo Viejo to have a drink. He felt entitled to a hot supper and a drink. His horse had won a race that day, and his livestock was safe on the savannah. He had won nice coin on Steeldust. He was getting ahead.

Long before sunup, Steeldust was awake and restless. He knew a monster with a tooth for agony and death was nearby. The whole thicket by Steeldust's corral reeked of decayed flesh and disease because the thing was pausing there to find which way to move next.

As the sun rose and the day warmed, the monster stayed near Steeldust in the shade of the thicket. Steeldust became frantic. He was too disciplined to try to jump the fence or run through it. He knew tearing at the fence would not save him. He ran inside his corral calling for help and nickering in warning. Mary and Placido thought he was calling to the mares in the field. The mares bunched together and stared at the thicket, trying to locate Steeldust's monster.

Mary went into the corral to quiet the horse. Steeldust ran by her and slid on his hind legs to stop between Mary and the thicket, scattering gravel into the brush. Mary haltered him and tied him to a tree in the corral. This did not quiet him. He kept lunging to the end of his rope and nickering.

The monster dozed and awakened to the sun that hurt his

sight. He watched Steeldust between fits of pain and fever that glazed his senses. Steeldust's presence comforted him. Steeldust's sound and motion gave him a bearing. For most of the past twelve hours his senses had been wrong, his body failing, because his brain was rotting.

The beast raised his eyes to Steeldust. Steeldust stamped the ground, bared his chest and screamed a challenge. The beast meandered through the thicket and came up behind Lindano. Lindano had come back to lie in the same thicket, so close to the corral that Steeldust had kicked gravel on him when he ran by Mary.

Lindano was grunting a prayer for help. He had lost his patience. He was being forced to pray. He could usually make anything happen without God, but he did not want to grovel any longer in thickets while he waited for a decision in his favor. He had hurried out that morning to force his luck and grab Mary and Steeldust, but Ursulo and his oxen had appeared early to plow a piece of the field near the *ramada*.

Now, Lindano lay on his belly praying that some Devil or God would come close to him and help him get what he coveted. Then, he heard teeth gnashing behind him, felt a hot breath on the calf of his leg, and his whole body went cold. The breath waltzed right up the ridge of his spine until it lifted the hair on the back of his neck. Again, the thing chomped and slobbered over its teeth, and in that instant a breeze shifted and Lindano smelled the stench of its mouth. He had been smelling dead flesh in the thicket and he thought some animal must have died near his hiding place, but now he realized the smell must be coming from the gangrene of some animal standing flush over his buttocks. He rolled to his back and looked straight into the face of the beast. A rabid coyote was standing so close to Lindano that he could have killed the man with the drip of slobber off one poisoned tooth.

Lindano left the thicket through the top, butting out

through the hardwood with his head, scrambling and claw-ing and holding his breath while he jerked his feet out of the coyote's reach. He hit the shallow water of the Rio Mayo running so hard he barely wet himself in crossing. He kept running in a straight line through the brush. He would have run all the way to Pueblo Viejo except he clotheslined himself on the limb of a *sanjuanico* tree. He brought himself down long enough to think of his horse and to pull his hat up off his ears so he could see.

Placido was carrying a bucket of water across the corral when the beast sauntered out of the thicket and blocked his way. Mary ran toward the *ramada,* and the coyote turned to look at her. Placido splashed him with the water, threw the bucket at him, and tried to run. The coyote caught the boy by the heel and brought him down. Steeldust tore loose from the tree and ran over the coyote, rolling him off Placido. He turned on top of him and began striking him with his front feet, stamping him, and dragging him away from Placido, but jerking his feet away to keep them clean.

Mary helped Cruz pick up the children and ran with them to Ursulo and the oxen. Steeldust planted himself and kicked the beast with both hind feet, then beat him out of the corral at the point of his hooves.

Ursulo, Cruz, Mary, and the children watched the coyote shamble away into the brush by the river. They saw that Steeldust had quieted down before they went back to the corral. The coyote had mangled Placido's leg. The coyote had used the spasms of snapping it uses to shock and break the back of small prey for an instant kill.

Mary used Steeldust's halter for a bridle, mounted him bareback, and ran for Marco, the *comisario.* She had to warn the community about the coyote and to find out where Placido could be taken for treatment. She had to control an irrational urge to push Steeldust faster all the time. That urgency could make her ride him to death. Steeldust's speed and power were of no use now. She did not want to run by Chihuahuita and miss it. She had never been there. She might not find Marco when she got there. She might have to look for him all day. A horse could be run to death that way.

Mary found Chihuahuita and then found Marco's house. His wife came out carrying a child on her hip, looking into Mary's eyes without expression as though she had known her all her life.

"*Señora,* a rabid coyote is wandering by the river," Mary said. "He bit Placido. We need Marco."

"He just left. He is not here," the woman said.

"Where? Which way?"

The woman stepped away from the front of her *ramada* and pointed to the trail Marco had taken. "He took himself that way," she said. "He can't be far away."

"Please tell the people to watch out for the coyote."

"*Sí,*" the woman answered. She used only a lisp in the intake of her breath to say the word. Mary tried to see into her face again, but the woman was looking away and dismissing herself. Mary felt close to her, but the woman was still politely hiding from her, denying that she knew this unfortunate American girl.

Mary let Steeldust hurry on Marco's trail, gambling she would find him before Steeldust tired. She rounded a bend in the brush and rode up behind a man riding a dark chestnut horse. Mary looked closely at the horse, trying to remember where she had seen him. He was so dark he was almost black. The man's shirt was torn. The skin on his back and shoulders was scratched and bleeding as though he had been rolled in the briars by his horse. The horse had a look in his eye that said he would like to do that to the man, and the man had a death grip on his reins. The horse looked well bred, though he was stringy and lank from hard use and he moved with a hitch in his flanks. The heavy hand of the rider kept his head perched too high for him to see where he was going, but he was going on, and his eye showed he was tough enough to carry any man to hell, and would go there gladly.

Mary hurried to pass the horse. The horse waved his head from side to side to keep sight of her and hurried to stay ahead. He backed his ears and switched his tail at Steeldust, threatening to kick. The man did not turn his head to look at Mary. Mary risked being kicked, and burst on by, crowding him into the brush. The man was carrying a *reata* with a loop ready in his hand. Mary did not look at the man's face.

Mary thought, "Is he after livestock? He looks like he's been towed through an acre of graythorn." Then she thought, "Does he think he's going to rope me?" Mary had been raised around cowboys and she had never seen one build a loop without intending to rope the first warm body that ran by. She heard the rope sing. She turned back and looked into Lindano's face just as the loop whipped out of his hand.

Mary laid over Steeldust's neck and shouted in his ear and he bounded away. The loop spread out and dropped off his hips. Mary looked back, and Lindano was goading Copper to run. Copper was lunging with his front feet, trying to climb up to the place where Lindano was holding his head. Lindano wanted him to run, but he was not going to turn loose of his head and maybe get bucked off. Mary shouted with laughter at the look on Lindano's face. He looked as though he thought he was doomed if he had to run for his life on Copper. His face showed that Mary had won the big jump that he most feared, and he was lost in any race against Steeldust. Steeldust soared away. Mary kept singing her laughter and looking back over her shoulder at Lindano. She had always wanted to go so fast she could look back and laugh at the Devil.

Then Steeldust was not soaring anymore. He was lunging, bogging, and flailing in brush because he had missed a turn in the trail while Mary was looking back. Mary looked to the front at a limb that was only a foot away, and too low for her to duck. She had not been forewarned. The limb swept her off her horse and she bounced off the ground, stunned.

Steeldust stopped, turned back, and stood by Mary in spite of the sound of Lindano's chortling, the sight of his horse-killing face, and the smell of the sweaty tallow on his ribs, as he caught up. Lindano caught Steeldust's tether, raised the chain quirt over Mary's head, and made her climb back on the horse. He led Steeldust away and laughed at the gloom in Mary's face. He headed for the edge of the world, his prayers answered by a rabid coyote.

CHAPTER 6

Horses are modest and fastidious by nature. By man's standards, they do not have disgusting habits. Their natures do not allow them to puke, whimper, or whine. When a horse is suffering, the basest sound he makes is a grunt, as if by making an effort he can rid himself of pain. Often, he will throw his head up and nicker, or scream his defiance or his intolerance of pain. On his own, he can bear his pain and live nobly with it.

The only time a horse might lose his modesty and fastidiousness in pain is when he is being whipped. The only time a horse might go running to the source of his pain for succor is when he is taking a whipping by a man. He will run back to the man who is whipping him for help, especially if the man has been keeping him in a pen so he could not eat, or exercise unless the man was good enough to come and open his gate.

The only kind of pain a horse cannot bear nobly is the kind man knows how to inflict. A man who trains his horses by whipping them operates on this principle.

PASCUAL and Bill rode in the alamo shade along the Mayo toward Chihuahuita. Bill did not know the country or the people. He had cowboyed farther south in the Sierra Madre, but he had only been as far south as Cajeme on the coast. He knew Pascual was near his family, though, and he had been told Mary and Steeldust were doing well with Cruz. Bill and Pascual had been stopping on the way and visiting with Mayo families, and they knew about the race between Steeldust and *Pluma Roja*. At each home, Pascual always told the stories of his adventures in the north since he had left

Sonora after the battle of Vicam. When he was finished, he was always told of the circumstances of his wife's escape from the Federal troops and about her return to the Maya. Then the story was told about the Steeldust horse and the blue-eyed girl called La Jineta.

The Mayos were making a legend of the story of the girl named María. She had brought the only blue eyes to the Mayo most of them had ever seen. Hers were the same eyes that were on the statues of Santa María in the churches. She and Steeldust had kicked dust in the faces of the cavalry, *La Cordada,* and various bandits and kidnappers in the Sierra Madre, from the United States border to the Mayo.

The Mayos said that Mary was a Texas girl who had been betrothed to a Texas man who had been killed when she was kidnapped. She escaped her kidnapper, and God brought her to the Mayo to give the people the *muestra,* the example of courage and horsemanship.

The seed of her Steeldust horse would someday make centaurs of every Yaqui and Mayo warrior. The Steeldust horse had carried Placido and Mary a hundred leagues and outstripped the *Yoris* through Arizona, Sonora, and the Yaqui and Mayo nations. He had bred a hundred Yaqui and Mayo mares along the way. Mary was called La Jineta—the horsewoman, the headlong child, the headlong horsewoman—by the Mayos.

When Bill and Pascual rode into Cruz's clearing, only Placido's mare greeted them. Bill looked for Mary, but only Pascual's little children came out to watch them dismount. Cruz called to Pascual that she could not come out. Pascual hugged his children to his legs and walked in. He found Placido feverish from the bites of the rabid coyote. Bill went in to shake hands with Cruz and was told that Mary had ridden Steeldust to find the *Comisario.* Chihuahuita was only a mile away, and she had been gone more than half a day.

Bill remounted Lizard and followed Steeldust's tracks to Chihuahuita. Marco's wife stepped away from the front of her home and showed him Mary's trail. Bill rode the trail to the bend in the brush where Mary had run into Lindano. He saw Steeldust's deep tracks and saw where he had stopped under the tree. He recognized Copper's tracks. He saw the clear imprint of Mary's hands in the loamy earth where she had fallen and helped herself up. He tracked Steeldust and Copper downriver through the thickets to the village of San Ignacio, where most of the region's trails converged. Marco rode up to stop him on a little flax-maned mule.

"*Ola,* can I be of service," Marco said.

"*Buenas,*" Bill said.

"Pardon me, but I never thought I'd see another Steeldust horse so soon. I was a lifetime seeing the first one. What is this one called? I am Marco, the *Comisario* of Chihuahuita."

"This horse is called Lizard—*El Lagarto*. I am Bill Shane, friend of Pascual Matus."

"Ah, yes, the Texan of Pascual."

Every gringo who wore a felt hat was a Texan to the Yaquis and the Mayas.

"Have you been to Pascual's home to see the boy who was bitten this morning?" Marco asked.

"I left Pascual there with his wife. Did the girl who rides Steeldust find you?"

"No, the people passed the word along the river. I've spent the day warning the people about the coyote with rabies. Now we can kill him. You have come here with your gun."

"I was hoping you had seen the girl and the big horse."

"I have. This morning in thick *monte* by the trail on this side of the river, I heard the *escupión,* the gila monster, coming. I hid as he went by. He was leading Steeldust and La Jineta, the girl you're looking for. I saw what he was doing and he did not see me. He was hurrying. This is a new way for him to act here. He's been slow to do harm here. We knew he was dangerous, but only if he was stepped on, or to someone who might stand carelessly too near his side. That's why we call him *El Escupión*."

"Are you talking about Lindano?"

"Yes. He has always been careful here and only done mischief when he thought no one was looking. Now he has irrigated it, *lo ha regado*, everybody in the country knows he is trying to get La Jineta to his wallow at Camauiroa."

"How far is it? Can I catch him before dark?"

"No, and you won't find him in the dark. He'll ambush you. The best you can do is to come back to Chihuahuita and help me hunt and kill the coyote. Stay and help me so Pascual can take his son to the doctor. In the morning, I'll show you the way to Camauiroa and you won't have to track El Escupión to find him."

"Show me now."

"Listen, Lindano will ride all day. He'll want to rest when he reaches Camauiroa. If you leave early tomorrow, you might catch him during his siesta. I know him. He'll rest on his beach all day tomorrow. If he wants to do mischief before that, you won't stop him by chasing him now. He'll think of mischief tomorrow evening."

"How do you know where he's gone?"

"Everybody knows that is where he takes women. He has taken various women out there, but until now they have all been whores. Last year, for example, he took Alma the prostitute. Before that he took other whores. They all returned safely, though worn. Don't worry, he doesn't know girls like María, La Jineta. That girl is innocent, courageous, and smart. She'll figure him out. She's not afraid of him, so all she has to do to keep him away is face him. An escupión can't bite anybody unless he becomes his companion, practically, and stands by his side."

Bill rode back to Chihuahuita and found that Pascual had taken Placido on the train to Guaymas. A delegation of *caciques* led by Ursulo were congregated at Cruz's *ramada*, waiting for Bill.

"Won't Pascual be recognized on the train or in Guaymas?" Bill asked Ursulo, after he had shaken the hand of every *cacique*.

"No," said Ursulo. "He rides third class with the Indians. The Indians will hide and protect him. The railroaders never recognize anyone. They want to keep their railroad running through the Mayo and the Yaqui. The trains can be easily stopped. Pascual will also be safe in Guaymas. Guaymas is Yaqui. In Guaymas, the aristocrats hide him. No one will know him there, either. His aristocratic friends, the Almadas and the Robinsons, will order a cure for the boy."

Cruz put out coffee for everyone. *"Café,"* she said, and went back under her *ramada*.

Ursulo's wife had come to help Cruz. She handed a cup of coffee and the sugar bowl to Ursulo. With a careful, steady hand, and a measuring eye, Ursulo lavished five spoonsful of Cruz's sugar upon his coffee. Stirring coffee and sugar together, he walked to the corral fence and examined Bill's saddle, handling each part of it as he scrutinized it. He sucked noisily at the rim of his cup and swallowed hard on the hot coffee, his fingers crooked elegantly away from the cup. As he finished, he swirled the remainder of the coffee to pick up the last of the sugar. He drained it, handed the cup back to his wife, and contemplated Lizard.

"I hear you call this horse Lizard, as though he had scales," Ursulo said to Bill. "This horse, like the other one, seems to come to us out of dreams. We don't know horses like these."

Bill did not feel like staring at Lizard and talking about him all evening. He wanted to talk about catching Lindano, even though he knew that raving about Lindano and running after him was not the wisest course. Bill forced himself to be polite. These people were trying to help him. All they wanted in return was for him to tell them about his horse.

"Is Lizard as fast as the other horse?" Marco asked. "He

must be. Placido told me Lindano tried to steal him too. He said Lizard allowed Lindano to ride him, but Steeldust would not let him ride. Why would Lindano want to steal a horse who would not allow himself to be ridden?"

"Lizard and Steeldust would nod side by side in any race, but Lindano always coveted Steeldust," Bill said. "Sometimes a man who can't handle a horse will do anything to own him so he can abuse him."

"This is a fine horse. I can see no faults in him. I guess you'll take this one with you when you go, too. Will you be bringing him back?"

"Most likely."

"Maybe we could have some colts from this one if you don't get the other one back. We would like to have colts."

"When I bring him back you can have the seed of Steeldust. You can't have Lizard's seed."

"A shame. I like this roan horse. We have no roans, even when we have other horses. We could keep a roan. The cavalry does not use roans, only solid-colored horses. We have been allowed to keep *Pluma Roja* because General Cazares gave him to us. We can't keep any other sorrel. The seed of the roan would be priceless to us, if he threw roan colts."

"If you could take seed from this horse, it *would* be priceless. He is *capón,* a gelding."

"No," Marco said, cocking his head at Lizard's flank, crouching to look at his parts. "No pumpers? Who would castrate such a horse?"

"No pumpers, only the hose."

"*¡Lástima!* What a shame! What brute made that decision?"

"Man is a brute. The man who owned him didn't want colts from Lizard."

A man stepped up to Marco. Bill knew him as the *amarrador* Alejandro, cohort of La Carbonosa, a horsethief who had tried to steal the High Lonesome horses at Cedar Canyon in Arizona during the cattle drive. Alejandro was one of the thieves who had escaped when Pascual caught La Carbonosa and hung him. Bill had known Alejandro on the Yaqui after the war, when Bill had worked for Cabezón Woodell. Alejandro saw that Bill was looking into his face and recognizing him, and he turned to Ursulo.

"I want this man's gun," he said.

"What for?" asked Ursulo.

"The coyote with rabies is in the thicket by my *ramada*."

"Ask the man."

"Where is the gun you carried at Cedros?" asked Bill. "The gun you used to shoot at us from the top of the canyon? Did you throw it away when you saw Pascual? Have you been going without a gun since then?"

"I don't want *líos*, disputes. The rabies is threatening my family. Give me your rifle." The man would not look at Bill.

"Show me the animal," Bill said. He took his rifle from its scabbard, walked out to follow Alejandro into the brush, and was followed by Ursulo and his delegation.

Alejandro's family was standing under their *ramada* by a fire. The woman and her children stood close together with the glow of the fire on their faces. Alejandro pointed into a thicket and stood back. Alejandro was as tall as Bill, and was sweating just as hard from the walk through the brush.

Bill walked around the thicket until he saw the beast. No breeze was blowing, and the stench was awful as he stepped closer to raise his rifle. The stink made him realize that the carcass was only a husk with madness inside to make it move. The derelict was standing as though in an act of death, an attitude for death. It was humped up with agony and poised between flying and collapsing and so alone with the business that not even an insect would touch it. Bill's .30-.30 slug blew the skull apart. The carcass made not a twitch or a sigh and did not bleed a drop, as though it had been dead long before it lost its stance.

Bill turned to walk back with Ursulo and the *caciques*. He saw Alejandro go to his family and stop at the fire with his back to Bill. He stood there and waited for Bill to be gone. He did not look at his family. The woman and the children had not moved.

Visitors came to sit quietly by Cruz's fire that night and listen to stories. Their main entertainment was storytelling. Now that Matus was back in the region, the legends would grow again. The people came to see Bill and Lizard and to listen to Bill, the very "Texan" who had raised and trained Steeldust. The story was engraved in forty memories and carried away to be retold a thousand times. Before Bill was ten days older, he would hear his own story repeated hundreds of miles from Chihuahuita.

At sunup the next day, Marco showed Bill the trail to Camauiroa and put him on Lindano's track. Bill spurred Lizard into the roughest, crudest, sidling lope ever known to man and hoped he would catch Lindano before it shook him loose from his bones. Bill had been using up his reserves for a long time. He had not rested since he left Pascual's mother's care at Canelas, and he was worn down again, but he ground his teeth and kept going. His wounds were stretching thin, but being a good horseman was saving him from being finished off by Lizard. He had never seen a horse who could make him want to go afoot, even down the street to a Saturday dance.

On the way to Camauiroa Mary made up her mind she would survive. When Lindano had first taken her, she wanted to live, no matter what kind of abuse she had to suffer. Now, she wanted to fight and survive with the dignity of the Mary who had run four hundred miles and then won a horse race on the same great horse. She would not submit to abuse and humiliation just so her carcass could go on functioning in the light of the world. She would not whimper or whine to any sonofabitch.

If Lindano was hoping to relish Mary begging him not to hurt her, he would be disappointed.

Mary knew her mother and daddy would probably prefer it if Lindano raped her and let her go, if his only alternative was to break her neck. Bill would want her to fight, though. She hoped he was coming after her. Where was he? She would sure be happy if he showed up sound, mean, and mad right about then. Whatever happened, she had made up her mind, La Jineta was going to give Lindano his money's worth when the fight started. Mary figured she had character enough to be damned mean when she was right. Copper was putting so many scabs and knots on Lindano's carcass he would not be able to outrun a fat woman when he dismounted. If Mary could and catch Lindano on foot for just a moment, she and Steeldust would be gone.

Mary brought herself back from that dream. She had no idea where she was, or which way to go if she got away. Lindano could track her until her tongue hung out. The longer he let her go, the easier she would be to handle when he caught her. All he had to do was let her run awhile and he could catch her with a drink of water, the way a cowman caught his wildest livestock.

Mary knew she better not anger him so he felt he had to manhandle her. If she could keep him tentative and unsure of himself, he might not be so dangerous. She decided not to shy away from him, but to keep facing him, confronting him. Then, maybe she could knock him out when he turned away to keep from looking her in the eye. He never looked her in the eye. She was certain that whenever he decided to make his grab for her, it would be when her back was turned. If she kept an eye on him, he might leave her alone. If he took hold of her and she struggled, her goose was cooked. She hoped, most of all, that he never came so close to her she had to smell his breath, but if he did, she wanted to make it the last breath he ever took.

Lindano stopped on the edge of a clearing, tied Steeldust's head high in a tree, and hobbled his front feet. He tied a rope between Mary's feet under Steeldust's belly and tied her hands. He walked to a *ramada* in the clearing, and one of the *amarradores* Mary had seen at the race came out smiling and rode away with him. While they were gone, Mary waited for the women in the *ramada* to turn toward her so she could call to them, but they would not look at her. Finally, she called to them, but they were resolved to ignore her and did not pause in their chores or look her way. She called again, and one came to her with a dipper of water. The woman held the dipper so Mary could drink, but did not look into her face. The sight of the woman walking away to her duties made Mary weep.

Lindano and the *amarrador* came back leading a mule packed with provisions and bedding. The *amarrador* smiled at Mary, took money from Lindano, and went back to his family. Lindano untied Steeldust, blindfolded Mary, tied the pack mule to Steeldust's tail, and led them away.

In late afternoon, Lindano became happy and talkative. He began whistling as they rode onto a long stretch of sandy beach. Mary knew when Steeldust began walking in deep sand, and she could hear the waves of the Sea of Cortez. Lindano dismounted at a weather-beaten set of pens by a spring of clear water, untied Mary, and removed her blindfold. He ordered her to gather firewood, while he cut brush with his machete and patched holes in the corral. He unsaddled Copper, unpacked the mule, put them in the corral, and gave them corn in morrals. Steeldust perked up his ears and whinnied for corn. He was not used to being denied his morral, his nose-bag. Lindano ignored him and pitched a tent. Steeldust nickered softly again to remind the man gently that he had not been given his feed.

"Yeah, you poor feller, Lindano's not going to feed you, so don't beg," Mary told the horse. "He's going to starve us so we'll appreciate him."

Cattle, too wild to drink with people around, were coming near the spring and waiting for a chance to water.

Mary built a fire and cooked supper. Lindano worked at

fixing his packsaddle. Mary replied quickly and clearly when
Lindano spoke to her. She looked him in the eye and showed
no sullenness. Horsemen, especially the bad ones, used
whipping as a punishment for a sullen and balky horse. Mary
did not want to give him the idea he could whip her. If he
ever took that chain quirt to her and did not kill her, she
would not let him live on the same earth with her.

Lindano ate his supper and said, "Now, first the horse."
He led Steeldust into the corral, hobbled his front feet
again, and tied one hind foot to the front feet. He sat in the
long shade of the corral, took off his big spurs, and put on
a pair of blunt cavalry spurs. He relaxed a moment on the
cool sand in the shade.

"This is fine," Lindano said, grinning. "I finally have you
both here. You're next, Missy." He mounted Steeldust,
jabbed him with the cavalry spurs, held the spurs tight into
his sides, and whipped him down his flank with the quirt.
Steeldust could not buck, and he could not fight, or even
obey the spurs and the quirt. He lunged, flailed with his
front feet, and fell on his side. A spur pierced his ribs when
he landed on Lindano's foot. He lay flat on his side, shocked
motionless by the spur impaled near his heart.

Mary picked up the biggest, heaviest piece of mesquite she
had gathered for the fire, and ran to bash in Lindano's skull.
She could not get into the corral without tearing at a pile of
brush on the gate. Lindano looked up and saw Mary coming
with her club and began wrenching and jerking at his leg to
get it out from under Steeldust. He slipped out of his boot
and freed the leg just as Mary reached him. He thrashed and
scrambled on his hands and knees with Mary swinging the
club at his head. He stood up, backed against the fence, and
drew his pistol. Mary swung the club at his head again. He
caught it, tore it out of her hand, and began to laugh. He
fired his pistol in the air, grabbed Mary by the hair, and
clenched it in his grip so tightly her eyes closed. He pulled
her to him and bit her on the mouth. He shoved her out of

his way, went to the spring for a bucket of water, and carried it back to the corral. Steeldust was still, his eyes glazing in the sun. Lindano untied him and splashed the water on his head, and the horse revived and stood up, wobbling.

The spur was still on the boot and sticking into Steeldust's side. Lindano laughed, put on the boot, tied Steeldust's feet together again, and tied his head snug to a post. He mounted and began beating Steeldust wherever he could land the quirt. He whipped him over the hips and made him lunge against the fence. He whipped him across his sheath and flanks until Steeldust's urine splashed on his hooves. He beat him on the neck until it began to swell with ruptured vessels. He wrapped the quirt over Steeldust's brow and the popper snapped in his eye. He grabbed the quirt by the poppers and bludgeoned the horse over both eyes with the butt.

He dismounted and untied the horse. He stood away from the horse, and Steeldust rushed to be closer to him, hurrying to see if he could please him and stop the whipping. Lindano held the tether and stepped away, and Steeldust hurried to him again. Lindano struck him with the butt of the quirt between the eyes and laughed. Steeldust laid his brow against Lindano's chest and gave out a little moan. It was a sound of sorrow that he had done so much to displease—without knowing what it was, held back as though afraid a loud complaint might also displease the man. Lindano laughed and slapped the horse's ears.

"Stand away, horse," Lindano said. "I'll let you know when I'm ready for you to come close to me again."

"You dirty son of a bitch," Mary said. "You moron. That horse never did anything in his life but find ways to help people. How could he know what *you* want? He's been doing a man's work. How could you expect him to be a horse for you?"

"He knows, or will know, or he'll die," Lindano said. "I'm about to educate him in Mahout's School of Good Manners. We'll see if he can buck and swim at the same time."

Lindano stripped to his shorts, unsaddled Steeldust, and mounted him bareback. He kept glancing at Mary to see if she was looking at his body. He started Steeldust toward the gate, and the horse stepped right out without offering to buck.

"Oh, so now you've decided you're a traveling horse, have you?" Lindano said. "Where shall we go? Let's go where *I* want to go."

Lindano ran Steeldust into the surf, showing off and whipping the horse over both hips by crossing the quirt over his chest. Steeldust launched himself into the waves, and Lindano wrapped the hand that carried the quirt into his mane to keep from being dumped on the beach. Steeldust had never known a beating before, and he wanted to be free of the man. Any time Lindano wanted him to go, he would go with all his might to avoid a whipping, especially if he could jump right out from under the man.

Lindano only had the halter rope and a mane-hold to help him keep his seat on Steeldust. The horse threw himself into the surf as though he intended to cross the Sea to Baja California. The first big wave swamped him just as he stepped into a deep hole. Lindano washed off his back and bounced on the bottom under the horse. Steeldust sprang for the surface and stamped on Lindano's foot, pinning him to the bottom. He jerked the halter rope away from Lindano and breasted another big wave as the man was surfacing. With his first swimming kicks, he caught Lindano in the chest with both hind feet. Lindano sank again, but while he was drowning, a capricious current carried him back to the beach. He came ashore, disarmed and vomiting seawater. The quirt was tangled in Steeldust's mane as he headed out to sea.

As he backed out of the surf and stood beside Mary, Lindano looked for Steeldust through the saltwater in his eyes. Steeldust was putting out to sea, braving the waves and swimming strongly. Mary was calling to him, and Lindano found his breath and began to call and whistle.

Steeldust ignored them. He may have been in an unfamiliar element, but he was making great headway. He headed west as straight as any captain could con his ship toward a new port of call. He swam on until he was so far away from Mary and Lindano they could not see him unless a swell raised him on the horizon. His ears kept working as he maintained his heading and watched for a place to land. One eye occasionally pointed back to make sure he was increasing his distance from the people. The other strained forward to puzzle over his bearing. He swam boldly and did not falter, and soon he would be out of their sight. He seemed to be sure his heading was right as long as he left the humans behind.

Mary began to weep quietly, heartbroken by the sight of Steeldust swimming away. Lindano was bawling, squalling at the top of his voice now. Three more swells and Steeldust would be gone.

Then, the horse turned back. He seemed to reconsider his bearings and he stopped going away. He came about and headed toward the beach, taking an angle that would land him away from the people. He had not been confused by the surf and lost his way. He had braved a sea to find a friendly beach.

As Steeldust swam closer, Mary saw the sea was roiling around him, and bodies were humping on the surface. Dolphins were circling the horse. They broke out of the water and cavorted in full view. They gave Lindano and Mary a good look at them, and then they sounded back into the sea. Steeldust had kept his composure, his ears flicking for his bearing, his injured eyes intent and calm, but the wind was roaring in his nostrils. He landed and walked ashore.

Steeldust came out of the Sea of Cortez a mad horse, growling. His nobility had made him try to get away and not hurt the humans. A good man had trained him and taught him to trust them and be gentle with them. Now the anger of a horse overwhelmed him, and he was just like his father, Red Duke the great stallion, protector of a generation of good horses. He was tired of the predator, tired of using his grace to avoid trouble, tired of letting the humans use him any way they wanted to. His muscles had become taut and stiff from the swimming and he could not see, but his anger drove him down the beach in search of Lindano. He could not run, but he could crawl like a tractor, and as he growled he dug his toes into the sand and hunted the beach for the man.

"The pig of the sea turned him back," Lindano said. His voice was husky from the squalling he had been doing. He rubbed his eyes with the heels of his hands. He squeezed his eyes shut, turned away from Mary, and poked their corners with his heavy fingers.

Steeldust homed in on the sound of Lindano's ugly voice and clumsily charged toward him. Lindano tried to move out of his path, but Steeldust heard his scrambling and adjusted his direction. When Lindano had done all he could to get out of the way and had become transfixed in the sand, Steeldust summoned all his momentum to run him over. Lindano whirled with his eyes as wide as he could hold them, his open mouth emitting squeaks, his arms reaching for safety, and his feet trying to free themselves from the sand. Steeldust began rolling the man end over end, somersaulting him in the sand. Each time Lindano opened his mouth to squeak, sand erupted from it and then filled up as Steeldust rolled his head into the sand again.

Then Copper nickered, and Steeldust, glad for a distraction from the business of trampling another creature, shambled away from the man. His muscles cramped, stiffened, and stopped him beside Copper. Mary hurried to him and saw that his anger had quit him as quickly as it had come over him. Steeldust was shaky and spent and wanting a friend, but he would not look toward Mary. She was searching for the trust she had always found in his eyes, but he would not look at her. Copper's call had made him forget his anger, but not his enmity of humans.

Lindano walked away and laid down in the tent. Mary gently took Steeldust's rope and tied him by Copper. "I guess the dolphins didn't want you in their ocean, Steeldust, so you're stuck with us again," Mary said. She watered him and gave him his morral. His left eye was clouded over from the beating. She knew she should take her club to Lindano's head, but she was no longer afraid of him. She felt she was as guilty as Lindano about Steeldust. She had been told by a good horse that she was no better than Lindano, because she was just another human being.

Mary walked back to the tent to make sure she knew what Lindano was doing. He had folded himself into the fetal position and was asleep on his bedroll. She thought of killing him, but she had to face the fact that she could not murder a man in his sleep, or any other way, for that matter.

She stayed in the corral with Steeldust that night. Lindano did not come out of the tent. She went to the tent in the early morning, and Lindano was still lying with his knees tucked under his chin as though he had not moved all night.

Mary built a big fire and put on water to boil in the coffee pot. She gathered Lindano's clothing, his boots, machete, crumpled old hat, and pocket knife, and fed it all to the fire. She put his .45 pistol in her belt. She looked for more clothing. The only garment left him was his shorts. Mary cooked herself breakfast and doctored Steeldust. He could barely walk. He would be no help to her in escaping. He was practically blind. He kept swinging his head from side to side, trying to see. His left eye was open and not as swollen as the other, but it was clouded over. She wiped lard over both eyes to protect them from the flies. His neck was swollen. He moaned when he took a step because of the spur wound near his heart.

Mary did all she could for the horse, then walked away and sat by the surf, watching the waves. While Lindano was sleeping she could saddle Copper and take the mule and leave. Lindano would not be able to follow her on Steeldust.

Without his clothes, Lindano would burn in the hot sun. She might escape him that way.

Before now, she had been sure that sooner or later someone would run Lindano down, hang him in a tree, and take her home. Now she knew no one was coming to help her, and since she was on her own she decided that leaving without punishing Lindano was no good. Why go away and leave him sound and whole now that she had disarmed him? She should at least take his tent away from him so sunburn would peel his hide.

Mary decided the only decent thing for her to do was shoot him. She did not have to kill him. She would just shoot his foot so he could not chase her. She began studying the pistol to see if she could learn to make it shoot. The .45 Colt automatic had so many safeties she could never learn to shoot it. If she figured how to lever a round into the empty chamber, unlatch the safety catch, and full-cock the hammer, she would never find the grip safety and learn to put the pistol in her hand properly.

Mary piled more wood on the fire. Something nagged at her. That she had taken the pistol away from him so easily bothered her. Why would he go to sleep and leave his pistol where she could get it? She looked up and caught him staring at her.

"Where's my trousers? Where's—?"

"Your gun?" Mary asked. "Here's your gun." She brought it to bear on his head, though she still did not know how to work it. Lindano's eyes went round and he swallowed hard.

"You're pitiful," she said. "I have your gun. I burned your trousers, your hat, and all the rest of your clothes. Now I'm going to shoot a hole in your foot."

Lindano watched the pistol. Mary did not know it, but anyone who carries a .45 pistol can tell when it is primed to fire just by looking at it. Lindano saw Mary was not even close to completing all the mechanics for shooting him in the foot. He relaxed and began to talk.

"I trusted you. You wanted me naked? You didn't have to burn my clothes. I'll stay naked for you as long as you want. You're too nice to shoot me, so don't point the pistol at me. You can't convince me you'll shoot. Your pistol isn't even primed to shoot."

She pulled on the trigger to see if some special grace would make it fire. As she suspected, the steel of the trigger resisted her. She tried to cock the hammer. Ironlike, it did not relent.

"Is that why you didn't shoot me, because you don't know how to shoot the gun? Shame, girl. How can you be my girl if you don't know how to make a gun go off?"

Mary glanced at the pistol, trying once more to fire it.

"Did you think my pistol would protect you against me? It won't shoot for you, so give it back. Take off your clothes, and let's do what we came here to do so you can go home."

Mary ran to the surf and threw the pistol into the sea. She turned to face Lindano and met the muzzle-blast of three shots fired over her head. He began reloading a revolver. He had kept a revolver hidden and had teased Mary by leaving an unloaded pistol for her to find.

"Get over here by me," Lindano said. "I won't beat you, or ruin your prettiness. I only want to ruin you a little for your husband. That part of you won't stay ruined, Missy. Satisfy me and you can go home."

"Yes, I'll satisfy you," Mary said. "As a corpse. Come near me and I swear, one of us will die."

Lindano dropped the pistol on his pillow and started moving toward her. Mary walked around the fire to keep it between them. The fire was enormous and hot with a heavy bed of mesquite coals. The sand outside the tent burned Lindano's feet. He tripped back into the shade of the tent and began looking for his boots.

He searched the tent until he was sure all his clothes were gone. When he came back out, Mary pulled a long, straight mesquite limb out of the fire. The end of it was glowing. She raked out part of the top of a boot so Lindano could see it.

"Here's your boot," Mary said.

"You think that bothers me? No, Missy." He lunged for her.

Mary waved the smoking limb at him. Lindano slapped it aside and rushed her again. Mary poked the firebrand into the hair on his chest. He began howling and slapping his chest. She pushed the firebrand against his breast bone. He flinched away, and Mary poked the coals into his open mouth. He slapped at the end of the limb to get it out of his face, then trapped it against the side of his face with the other hand. Mary jerked it away and whacked his head with it, and sparks showered his head and shoulders. He caught it with both hands, and she dropped it and ran. He threw it away and scratched frantically at the sparks in his hair. Mary picked up the coffee pot, ran right back, and dashed the boiling water on his belly. She ran into the tent, and he plunged after her with his head still afire.

Mary knocked down the tent pole, and as the tent collapsed, she dove to escape under the back side. She planned to brain him while he floundered in the tent. She had placed a big, round rock behind the tent for the purpose of bashing Lindano's head. Lindano caught her ankle and stopped her before she got out. She whirled on him and smashed his snuffling nose with the heels of both hands. That blow and his fight with the sparks in his hair made him roll away from her. Mary groped for daylight. She found the edge of the tent and felt the fresh air on her face. She sensed a footfall near her hand. She reached out and touched a boot. Someone gently lifted her hand and held it. She jerked it away.

Bill had followed the tracks of Steeldust, Copper, and the mule down the beach until he saw the tent and the big fire. He hid Lizard in the brush and moved up behind the corral. At first he did not recognize the horses. Copper had been in better flesh, and his color was chestnut sorrel when Bill last saw him. Now he was black. The other big, gaunt sorrel looked familiar as Bill walked up behind him. The horse became aware of Bill and started, but he was too sore to jump. He turned a clouded eye to Bill with an anxious look that showed he was afraid of new abuse by the skulking human. The horse looked ill, as though he was infected with distemper, or tetanus. His neck and eyes were so swollen the skin was shiny and tight. Matter flowed from his nose, and flies crawled over his eyes and muzzle. Bill stopped in his tracks when he recognized Steeldust.

Then, Mary backed away from the tent, picked up a mesquite club, and began whaling on Lindano. Bill watched her deal him a beating, branding, and scalding. Bill hurried to the battleground after the tent collapsed. Lindano's howls told him Mary was holding her own. Her grunts and growls showed she had zeal for the fight with Lindano.

Bill was wearing his pistol, but he did not draw it. He could not shoot Lindano until somebody came out from under the tent. He walked by a pile of bones. The remains of a shark's jaws and teeth yawned at him as though they had been exposed in their grave. He picked them up, hefted them, and walked on. They were heavy and still covered with rotten meat and hide. He almost stepped on Mary's brown hand when it emerged from under the tent. He did not pull her out from under the tent when he picked up her hand because she jerked it away from him. The sight of Mary's little hand, burned and made smaller by the trouble Lindano had caused her, made Bill crack the shark's jaw against the ground so Lindano would move his head under the tent, and give Bill a target.

Lindano and Mary were fighting to get out from under the tent. Bill circled them and struck at Lindano's head, trying to learn the best way to handle the jawbone as a weapon. The teeth began to rattle and loosen in his hand.

Mary scrambled out, ran toward the ocean, and stopped.

Lindano jumped up under the tent suddenly and butted Bill under the chin before Bill could get out of the way. Bill lost his grip on the jawbone as Lindano trampled over him.

Bill had bitten his tongue and he felt some of his own teeth were shattered. Lindano tore loose from the tent, his eyes wide. Bill was trying to pick himself off the sand. Lindano raised Mary's big rock over Bill's head. Mary snatched up the jawbone and began screaming as she ran at Lindano. Lindano turned to look at her and saw the jaws begin their descent toward his head. He threw down the rock and ducked. The rock grazed Bill's forehead, smashed his nose, and crushed his hand against the ground.

Mary brought the jaws down on Lindano's head, and they caught around his neck as she lost hold of them. He ran for the corral. Mary scrambled to find Lindano's pistol. She knew how to shoot a six-shooter. A baby could shoot Lindano with a six-shooter. Lindano was mounting Copper. Bill could not see. He was full of pain again and squirming on the sand with his pistol underneath him. Mary scrambled over the top of him, still looking for Lindano's pistol. She looked up and saw Lindano take hold of Steeldust's lead.

Mary had jammed the shark's jaws over Lindano's head and they fit tightly around his neck. They had opened when they went on and shut when Mary lost hold of them. The drying flesh and sawing teeth made them impossible for Lindano to remove while in a hurry to get away.

Mary saw the six-shooter sticking out of the sand by the fire. She dove for it, snatched it up, shook it, blew sand off it, cocked it, pointed it, fired, and chipped the top off a fence post twenty feet from Lindano. She ran toward the corral gate while she cocked the six-shooter again. She reached the gate as Lindano was coaxing both horses through. She set herself, aimed at Lindano's head, and exploded a round that grazed his brow with the muzzle blast, knocking him over. He caught himself against Steeldust, who was pressing against Copper as they passed through the gate. The explosion of the six-shooter, close under the horses, stampeded them. Lindano looked back over his shoulder at Mary as though dismayed by the way she was acting.

Copper was in a panic because Steeldust was stumbling along and anchoring him in the range of the six-shooter. Mary sighted along the barrel of the six-shooter, fired again, and missed. She kept firing and missing until she ran out of bullets, but not before she had scared Copper and the exhausted Steeldust into a runaway that carried Lindano far out of range.

Bill raised his head in time to see Lindano leave with his horse again. He bowed his head over the tent and watched his blood make a puddle under his face. He could not lift himself any higher, just high enough to keep his face out of the puddle. Mary knelt beside him.

"Have you got any bullets that'll fit this thing?" she asked. Bill did not answer.

"You'd better get after him if you have a horse and a gun. If you don't have a horse, I have a mule."

"He can't get away. He's surrounded by water," Bill said. He raised his head because Mary's voice had a smile in it. She brought her face around, found his mouth, and kissed him.

"Glad to see you," she said softly. "How the hell did you find me?"

"A sonofabitch leaves big tracks."

"I never dreamed you'd get here in time. I was just about to conk him with the same rock he dropped on you."

Mary put both arms around Bill's shoulders and began to weep. Mary's face was close to Bill's. She smiled and laid her head on him. He was using his bandana to stop his nose from bleeding. Her tears were warming him through his shirt.

Mary took the bandana off her head, wet it in the surf, and began cleaning Bill's face. "I bet you hurried down here because you were worried I was petting your horse. I bet you worried about that as much as you worried old Sheep Dip was hurting me."

"Am I wrong, or wasn't he stark naked when he left here?"

"He wasn't *stark* naked, but naked enough so I was able to scald him all over his raping gear."

"How did he get so naked?"

"He thought I wanted to look at him, so he just couldn't wait to take off his pants."

"I guess he didn't get what he wanted. He left you fully dressed with a club in your hand."

Mary smiled, and Bill squeezed her, sighed, and lay down on his back. Mary began examining him. His hand and fingers were mangled. His nose had swollen until his eyes, brows, and cheekbones were on the same plane.

"You'll be so ugly I'll be the only girl you can bribe with your horse, from now on," Mary said.

"I have to get the horse back before I can give him to you," Bill said. "How's my credit?" He reached for Mary's waist. He had been thinking of her waist since it slipped inside his hands during her rampage in the cholla. She was thinner now, but the tips of his fingers touched her warmth there, just the same.

"Good," Mary said.

"What?"

"Your credit's good. Your horse already saved my life."

"Poor old thing. He's sick, too. Has distemper or something, doesn't he?"

"No, Lindano beat him half to death."

Bill felt the rage welling. He tried to speak, but could not. He just put his arm over his eyes. He wanted to be after Lindano, but he had come to a full stop.

"I better go get my horse and water him," Bill said.

"What horse are you riding?"

"Old Lizard."

"Lizard? I'll be glad to see him."

Mary was lying on his chest with her face in front of his. "Kiss me, I'm awful happy," she said. "Do you think I'm grown up now?"

"A lot, Mary."

Mary kissed him, and Bill patted her and stood up to make himself get going.

After they took care of the animals, Bill and Mary made love. They told each other all the secret thoughts and dreams they had been waiting to share, if they ever got the chance to be alone. They knew they would be separated at least once more. Their scars kept reminding them.

The next day, they rode Lizard double and led the mule back to Cruz's ramada, and every time they looked at each other they smiled.

Bill bought provisions at Chihuahuita and rested with Mary that night. Cruz attended them and fixed them an alcove with *petate* mats in a corner of the crowded *ramada*. Mary doctored Bill and slept with her head on his shoulder. The Mayos held vigil and council in their soft voices by firelight through the night.

Bill went to the corral early. He knew he had to keep moving or he would find excuses to stay with Mary. He wanted to get after Lindano now and bring his horse home. He saddled Lizard and packed one of Marco's mules. Mary packed coffee, beans, and jerky and cooked a lunch for his morral.

Bill and Mary did not commiserate or say how much they wanted each other. They stayed under the cover of their chores and went on with the business they were staying in Sonora to finish. They respected the Mayos, and the Mayos expected Bill to go after his horse, and Mary to wait with Cruz and not cry and carry on because Bill was leaving. Bill and Mary were like the Mayos: they did not think it was right to waste time when a man's horse had been stolen and abused.

Bill was on his way to Camauiroa again at sunup. That ride—to find Lindano's tracks again—was the longest of his life. All the pains Mary's touch had taken away came back to hurt him as he retraced the route he and Mary had taken the day before.

He found Steeldust's tracks easily and slowed down to follow them. The chore of tracking Steeldust would make Bill ride twice as slow as Lindano. He hoped Lindano would stop to find shade and clothes and wait for Mary's brands to heal and the hair to grow over his hide again.

Lindano did not run far. As soon as he was out of sight and range of Mary's pistol, he pulled up. Being naked and bareback and leading the plodding Steeldust, while Copper was trying to run out from under him, was just too hard on him. Steeldust seemed to be totally blind. He kept coming to a dead stop in the brush and loosening Lindano's bare seat on Copper.

With no saddle to hold his rump in place and no spurs for his bare heels, Lindano's seat was always sliding. His bad luck put him on the verge of weeping. The girl had lighted a fire on him and run him off without even his clothes to protect him. He had striven with wholesale effort and desire, planning, and even prayer to make this kidnapping enterprise a success. He had been rewarded with nothing more than a blind horse. The enterprise was ruined.

Now Copper's gait was ruining his body. Mary had seared and scalded him on all his upper surfaces, and Copper was galling him on his bottom surfaces. The sun was braising him evenly from the bald spot on the top of his head to the hair on the top of his toes. One surface way back on his tailbone was sound enough to support his weight on the horse, but he could not use it because he had to bend forward at the waist to keep from stretching the skin on his blistered belly. In that position, Copper's prominent backbone ravaged him mercilessly.

Lindano reached the *ramada* of the *amarrador* Alejandro that evening. Alejandro found him clothes so he could dress as a *vaquero* again. He doctored his own sores with soda and lard and bought a saddle that he had to pay too much for. He rode on toward the Sierra Madre the next day. He needed rest, but rest with Bill Shane on his trail might turn into the eternal sleep. Alejandro did not encourage him to stay and did not offer to ride with him to help him, either.

Three days after he left Camauiroa, Steeldust began falling. He stumbled with every step and held Lindano to a walk. Stress made his nose bleed, his voice grunt, his breath roar.

As Lindano rode close to the canyon in the Sierra Madre where he planned to leave Steeldust, he looked back at the horse with satisfaction. He finally had a fine horse suffering all the misery and degradation he could endure. He had always wanted to do that to a horse, and he had done it to the best horse he ever knew. Now it was time to see how much abuse the horse could take. A little starvation and loneliness would school him so Lindano could begin his retraining.

Lindano reached a high, narrow ridge above a box-canyon called Ojo de Agua. He felt sad as he looked down into a clear blue eye of water that pooled off a high waterfall into the bottom of the canyon. The blue of the pool reminded him of Mary's eyes. He would probably never see her again. He had not won her, after all.

Graythorn *vainoro* choked the entrance to the canyon. Lindano dismounted and led the horses through a tunnel in the brush that ranchers had cut with machetes. An immense *chapote* tree grew beside the pool and its boughs touched both rims of the canyon. The place was haunted by dangerous predators. The people of the region respected Ojo de Agua as a good watering place. Once in a while someone would trim away the brush in the entrance so livestock and pack trains could trail in to water, but as a rule it was shunned as a deadly place. Lindano knew, if he barricaded the entrance, the people would know someone was holding livestock there and leave Steeldust alone. He released

Steeldust under the *chapote* and slapped him over a blind eye to make him turn away.

"Now, bigshot horse, you can stay in my dungeon alone," Lindano said. He was cranky and unsmiling and he could not understand the reason. He was still having his own way, to a degree. He kept talking to Steeldust to see if he could put himself in a better mood.

"See how you like it in a pit, waiting for the beasts or the vermin to come and eat you. Maybe an old snake will come sleep with you tonight. Maybe a spoiled old jaguar who is too slow to catch his meat regularly will smell you and come get you. Maybe a rabid skunk will come up behind you and spoil your peace. Stay here all by yourself until you're sure no one will ever come for you. You'll never see another horse again.

"Let's see how you make it with plenty of deep water for swimming, but no pigs of the sea to turn you back and keep you from drowning. You're a glutton, so you will eat all your feed the first week. After that, you won't need to eat because there is nothing in here for you to do. You'll be happy to see me coming, if I ever come back this way.

"You and that girl ruined me and I need some time to heal. I'm not superhuman, you know. When I return, this canyon will have brought you to my service. I'll ride you out of here, if you're not dead. My patience has limits, you know. I can't do everything for you. I've done my best to make you a better horse. You'll heal, but I don't want to look at you while you do it. I want to remember you just the way you are, while I go far away and people forget me."

Lindano stacked brush in the entrance and rode away almost comfortably because he was no longer towing Steeldust like an anchor. He felt he had handled himself well. He had gambled for the highest stakes: great wealth and a young life. He had lost the pleasure and the money he would have won with the girl, but he still had the horse. The cauldron of Ojo de Agua would render the horse's obstinancy away like tallow. Lindano rode toward Chihuahua still grieving for Mary's blue eyes. Now, there, he had lost too much.

When Steeldust could no longer hear or smell Copper, he knew the black-hearted man was gone. He moved one joint at a time until he touched the canyon wall. He found himself standing in fresh, running water and leaning against cool rock. His world was blood red. His left eye lay in agony in its socket. He raised his head and called for his own kind, but he could hear no answer.

The cold water began to soothe the aching in his feet and legs. He found sweet grass in the rock by his side. He nudged it with his upper lip, nibbled it, bit it off, and chewed it carefully until he was able to swallow. He grazed until night, standing carefully so his legs could rest; he savored his peace, the green feed, and the fresh water. Alone and blind, he could not have found a better place. The dust of centuries had filled all the pitfalls in the loamy ground.

The next morning, he forced his eyes open and found he could see with his right eye. The glow of the sun brightened the veil on his left eye. Then, a tiny white spider on the catch of a breeze, loosed his thread and glided to Steeldust's face. He busied himself exploring the eye to see if Steeldust's terrain was suitable for his work. Tiny as he was, each time he flew on his silk he was carried into some new chaos, the nature of which he must quickly understand, or perish. He liked the crags and brush and climate of Steeldust's sorest eye. He began to work, anchoring, lacing, and streaming his web over the hurting eye, outlining the designs of his toil over the throbbing place.

The web of the tiny white spider was shield, filter, and salve for Steeldust's eye. The horse was grateful for the spider's company, though the spider was no bigger than the head of a pin. Steeldust waited by the hour for the spider to move across a tender spot so he could be sure that he was still there. The spider caressed the eye with his business, and he was the only friend who came to touch Steeldust with concern in his loneliness. The white spider's touch had the power to soothe and heal, though his legs were smaller than Steeldust's lashes. On awakening, and before he ever moved, Steeldust always marked the whereabouts of his friend. He knew each time the little fellow marched over his face, and the spider's gentle work kept him in a good humor.

CHAPTER 7

The Mexican charro professes that in his life a man should claim only one God, one country, one woman, and one horse.

BILL looked up from Steeldust's tracks at the black clouds. The first drops of an *equipata*, an equinoxal rain, began to wet him down. He loved rain, but the *equipatas* could cause the country to flood. He was sure to lose Steeldust's tracks.

Bill kept riding and put on his slicker. He would never be able to deal with Lindano if a little rain made him flounder and hunt for shelter. In this country Bill was home, and he could stop at any ranch and be welcome. Lindano would soon be crying for his mama, because no one in this part of the Sierra Madre would help him. Lindano had made his last mistake when he chose this region for a place to hide. This was country that Bill knew better than any Yankee and as well as most of the natives.

Not an hour would pass without someone seeing Lindano and Steeldust on the trail. Steeldust and Copper might not leave tracks in running rainwater, but their presence was being noted everywhere they went. To hide all that horseflesh in this country, he would have to be stealthier than a snake.

Bill had first ridden in the Sierra as a twelve-year-old buying cattle with his father. Later, he came to recuperate when he was released from the Marine Corps after the war. He spent a year prospecting for placer gold, then he went farther north to help Cabezón gather his cattle. He had not been back to the Sierra since he started working for R.E.

Bradford, but he bet he had more friends there than the Pope.

Bill had become feverish, and he often rode along in a delirium. To concentrate, he thought of Mary's face. He could remember it as clearly as though her picture were on his saddlehorn. Before Camauiroa, he had only been able to recall the way she looked when she was uncomfortable, like when she looked away when she chewed as though she was afraid she might offend someone by the way she ate. He was always moved when he watched her eat because it made her seem somehow vulnerable, childlike. He was sorry the task embarrassed her.

He remembered all Mary's weaknesses. She was a weak runner. He remembered her running toward him once when she was fourteen. She felt, all of a sudden, that she was exposing too much of herself. She dropped all her conceits when she ran. She had smiled and stopped running when she saw Bill watching her.

Now, since Camauiroa, Mary's face was easier to remember. She was smaller and leaner, calmer and prettier than the former Miss Mary who had always been surrounded by rich parents, roadsters, schoolmates, and her "things." The horseback trail from Red Rock showed as lines in her face now. The lines that moved Bill most were the good-humored ones alongside her nose. They were from smiles but had been drawn during her trouble. She might as well have come along to track Lindano with him. She was stouter-hearted, healthier, and probably stronger than Bill, now. Even the big horse had not come through the trouble as soundly and strongly as Mary.

The slicker was making Bill hot. Sweat ran around the edges of the scabs on his face and pooled against his skin under his clothes. He had some mescal Ursulo had given him, and he was rationing it. He caught himself slumping in his saddle once in a while but he always made himself straighten up. He was not going to let Lindano ride him down. He was in his own country.

Water stood everywhere in the flats and was running in the trail. Steeldust's tracks were underwater. Bill headed for *El Desengaño,* a glade by a stream. He had spent months prospecting there, alone, after he came back from the war. As he rode into the glade the rain splashed on the surface of the stream so hard it seemed to stop it from flowing. The rain was cold. The stream was rising without seeming to flow. Bill cut brush and built his lean-to where it had been before. He started his fire with dry wood from a rat's nest that he remembered. He unsaddled Lizard, carried his pack and panniers from the mule, and made his camp comfortable before dark. He ate the last of the lunch Mary had prepared for him. He saw to the tether and hobbles of Lizard and the mule tied to a *tepeguaje* tree. The trunk and lower limbs of the tree were still smooth from use he had given it. He unrolled his bed under the lean-to, pulled off his boots, allowed himself a glowing swallow of mescal, and climbed into his blankets.

Bill's camp was across the stream from the main trail. Bill tried to stay awake, but he began to nod. He unbuttoned his shirt and trousers and lay still. Light drops of rain spattered on his tarp over the lean-to. The night was dark as the inside of a rain barrel. Winter would begin right after this rain. His pain calmed, and he slept.

During the night, Bill heard the bell mares of a pack train moving south on the trail. The *arrieros* talked to their animals in soft and urgent voices. Horseshoes rang on the rock. The sounds were clear because the rain had subsided. Bill was lying so he could see across the stream where the pack train was passing, but the darkness was absolute. He thought he could see sparks fly as the horseshoes glanced over rock. The *arrieros* kept their voices low, as though they were aware of Bill's peace and would wait to pass his camp before they raised them again.

Bill figured the train must be carrying contraband to be moving so late on that kind of night. An *arriero* began whistling a tune Bill had never heard and knew he would not remember. He loved Mexican tunes. He had been accused of being the prime backer and financier of the poorest mariachis of Sonora, even when they should have been allowed to starve. He had not only supported good mariachis who played well and stayed sober, he had paid overwhelming gratuities to tone-deaf mariachis like the ones called Los Ciegos, three congenitally blind brothers who carried into the bordellos music that was like the theme for original sin.

The whistling meant the *arrieros* knew his camp was there, and they were making music to put him at ease, as was the custom. Bill wondered how they knew his camp was there. He sipped mescal and relaxed. He enjoyed the sounds of men working on the trail while he was lying at ease in bed where he belonged. When the pack train had passed, he slept again.

Rain awakened Bill at dawn. The stream had risen to the edge of his lean-to. He went out to feed Lizard and the mule, then built a fire and put on his coffee pot. He rolled and tied his bed and sat on it while he heated jerky, beans, and *gordas* Mary had packed. He packed the mule and saddled Lizard. Standing in the rain, he said a prayer while they finished the corn in their morrals, remembering the saying *Por oir misa, y por dar cebada, no se pierde la jornada.*—The time taken for hearing mass and graining your mount, is not time lost in the journey.

Bill did not have to track Lindano anymore. He could make better time by riding fast and talking to the people. The storm was helping Lindano because fewer people would see him, but his trails were more limited as he rode higher in the Sierra.

Bill rode south in the same direction as the pack train and noticed the rain had wiped out its tracks. Bill's own tracks had been plain enough to see at El Desengaño. He marveled that the rain had spared some of his tracks from the evening before but had washed away every sign of the pack train that just passed across the stream. He rode on, trying to remember the tune the *arriero* had been whistling. The tune had been suitable for a night march. He hoped to remember it and use it when he rode at night, but it was too beautiful and complicated to recall.

Once before in his life Bill had been awakened by a beautiful song, the time he heard the song of the porcupine. He had never been able to describe it, and no one else in the world had ever described it, so far as he knew. No one ever believed Bill when he told them about being privileged to hear the porcupine's song, so he had begun to doubt it himself. Once in a while, among friends, he spoke wistfully about the night he heard the porcupine sing in his camp at Moon Lake, Utah. The song of the *arriero* had been like that, so delicious it must have tasted good on the man's tongue.

Bill stayed on the trail all day in the rain and met only one man. He knew the dried-up, little man who was hurrying toward him, but he did not want to acknowledge that he did. He did not want to stop and talk about their friendship, only about Lindano. The man gauged the distance between them, and the width of Bill's animals, so he would know where to get off the trail to let Bill pass. He glanced quickly at Bill's eyes to give Bill a chance to exchange greetings, but he was in a hurry to give Bill the right of way and go on.

"*Ola, compañero,*" Bill said. The man stopped and looked longingly down the trail past Bill. He marked the spot his next step would fall and then looked in Bill's eyes and quickly examined their condition and their humor.

"*Ola, ola, ola,*" the man said quickly, to get the salutation over with. His homemade palmetto hat was soggy and bearing down on his ears. He had to tilt back his head to look out from under the brim at Bill.

Bill did not want to notice the man now, how his clothes were heavy with water, while his face was dry as dust, how old he had become. He had always been a good friend, but Bill had no time for him now.

"Is Lindano on this trail?" Bill asked.

"Si, señor. I saw him yesterday. Was it yesterday? Day before yesterday. Before the rain. With the Estíldos."

"How did the horse look?"

"*Andando, no mas. No mas andando.* Just walking."

"What condition was he in, man?"

"Listen, Señor Bill, you see me standing here. Don't you think I must lack judgment? How would I know about the condition of a horse? I don't even know better than to endanger myself by walking long journeys in the rain."

"Is Don Alfredo Almada at home with Doña Elena and are they well?"

"Yes, they're home, they're well."

"Thank you. Pardon me for detaining you, though I'm glad to see you after all these years, Manuel." He *finally* remembered the man's name.

"No, no, no. Don't concern yourself. I should beg your pardon. I don't even know where I am or what I'm doing out in this rain."

"Go. Get inside, Manuel"

That evening, Bill stopped at the home of his friend, Don Alfredo Almada, the mescal maker of Cochibampo. He had been promising himself he would stop there for mescal and Doña Elena's healing. She was a gifted healer, *sobadora* and *curandera*. In sight of the house, Bill began to whistle the song, "Panchita."

Don Alfredo was in his corral, squatting with his head against a cow's flank, milking. The rainstorm muted Bill's sounds, but he knew Don Alfredo heard him. The old man kept his hat pressed into the cow's flank until he had stripped her of her milk. He stood up and untied the hobbles from above her hocks. He smiled at Bill, gave him his hand, and handed him the milk bucket.

"Pardon me, old friend, for not attending to you sooner,

but I wanted to give you a swallow of warm milk." He watched Bill, afraid he might fall off his horse. Bill was about to collapse. He sat on his horse, held the milk bucket, and looked dumbly at Don Alfredo. He had come to a stop again.

"Is this you, Bill, whom I've known since he was a *buqui*?" Don Alfredo asked. "Now that I look in your face, I'm not sure who you are. I expected to know you after five years, and I do. But not even your own father would recognize you, unless he had known you were coming, as I did.

"You need rest and food. Start with a big swallow of the milk. Mescal has probably been keeping you moment by moment, but milk, tortillas, beef, and chile are what you need now. They're saying that you've been riding in a trance, talking to your horse, ignoring your friends on the trail. People have been passing you with a prayer instead of a salutation."

"What people?" Bill asked with a moan. He did not press for an answer. He sipped at the edge of the foam on the bucket. He stayed on Lizard because he did not know how to detach himself. He watched Don Alfredo finish his chores. Was it true? Had he been delirious? Could he remember every step he had taken that day? How much time had he taken to ride from El Desengaño? He had been using that trail since he was twelve years old. Had he seen it all again that day? He did not think so. He looked for manure dust or mud on the foam of the milk. The foam was clean. The old bucket was so clean it shone.

"You're a good milker, Don Alfredo," Bill said. "No trash on your milk or smears on your bucket. How do you do that in the rain and slop?" Bill knew how he did it, he only wanted to give him a compliment to show he was still sane.

"It's the same as urinating, son. After seventy-five years controlling so small a stream and calculating its fall twice daily, you learn to keep clean and hit the mark. What else can a man learn to do well? If a man can't milk a cow or pee without making a mistake after seventy-five years of practice, what dignity can he claim?"

Don Alfredo helped Bill dismount, unsaddle Lizard, and unpack the mule. In the house, Doña Elena patted him with a soft hand she had just washed but had not dried. She just squeezed the water off one hand with the other. She made him sit and gave him a supper of hot milk and coffee, honey, tortilla, and butter.

"Won't you eat with me?" Bill asked. Don Alfredo was sitting across the table from him, smoking home-grown *macuzi* tobacco rolled in a corn leaf.

"We require little fuel at night," Don Alfredo said. He held the long, fat, corn-leaf smoke between thumb and forefinger in front of his face so he could watch the ember. He was looking out the window at Lizard.

"Lindano started coming here five years ago, after you left," he said. "You and your father had brought us knowledge, jobs, friendship, commerce. Some of us welcomed Lindano, because we hoped he would do for us what you had done. He did not. He disparaged us, cheated us, and became our enemy in less than a year.

"What a change of fortune now, for our worst enemy to be driven here by our best friend. *¡Que casualidad!* What a coincidence of bad fortune for Lindano.

"Each time he left here, we hoped something would get him before he came back. We never thought we would be lucky enough to see you run him up a tree where we could watch the finish."

"Believe me, he's not running from me. He's running from La Jineta. Look at my face and hands. The last time I saw him, he dropped a rock on me and he probably thinks I'm still under it. La Jineta was the one who put him in the breeze. If you saw him go by here, you were witnessing the ancient fear a coward has for a fierce woman. The girl I call my *novia* is a girl they call La Jineta. She's called that because of her horsemanship, but also because she can be as fierce and sharp as a lance. Lindano must have a boil on his buttock, or some pocket of poison in him, that makes him so mean. Mary is a lance aimed at that boil."

"We know about the girl, even here. La Jineta is famous. So, it's true she is your intended, your *novia*? Tell us about her."

"She's no prim little thing waiting for her betrothed, arranging herself and all her little contracts so she'll be acceptable as a bride. She is the one Lindano is afraid of. If she were here she wouldn't require cow's milk to go on. She would be sharpening the lance she is named for.

"Lindano and I have faced each other three times. I took him by surprise the first time, had him down, and could not hurt him. He has had me down twice, and he almost killed me both times. I dealt him my best blow with a pair of spurs and couldn't even split his lip. He shot me twice and hit me deep with both bullets. He bashed my head with a rock this last time. La Jineta faced off with him once and she stripped him, disarmed him, clubbed him, branded him, and put him in the breeze with his hide smoking."

"We've heard that story, even here in the Sierra. You were too good to him, Bill. You must have struck him with love, not with hate. Charity held your hand, did it not?"

"Ah, Lord, I hope I'm given another chance to hit him, then. He keeps eluding me, and he has my horse. I think I must be trying too hard because I need so much to stop him. I'm sorry, but maybe I hate the man too much."

"You're unfortunate to hate a man, yet be unable to harm him. To have the use of two such horses as Steeldust and Lizard, yet lose the one you most esteem and not appreciate the other."

"You think I don't appreciate Lizard? Why?"

"Look at him."

Bill looked out the window. Lizard's sides were so gaunt his ribs were sticking out. His nostrils were still flared and blowing steam two hours after he had been put away. New sweat flowed over old on his hide. The mule was lying in the rain in a sloppy corner of the corral. Both had stopped in their tracks where they had been unsaddled. Neither had moved to take shelter under the *ramada* in the corral, because they were so tired.

"My God, who has been using my animals?" Bill asked.

Don Alfredo looked at his wife. "I've heard of such men, horsemen, who could kill a good mount chasing an enemy, men like Lindano, unfortunate men. Disgraceful that two such men are riding your horses, the best horses this country has ever seen. Two days ago, Lindano led your horse by here in the same kind of hurry. He was riding a horse almost as fine as your horses, and he'll kill him too."

Bill did not want to sit and examine how bad he had been, or how unfortunate he had become, or how disgraceful his hurried pursuit had become.

"Don Alfredo, what was the pack train carrying that passed me on the trail last night?" Bill asked. "It must have come by here about noon today."

"Son, no pack train passed here today. You're the only traveler from the north."

"No, Don Alfredo. They came this way. They could not have gone another way unless they left the trail and climbed the cliffs on both sides, or flew."

"They flew. None passed here."

"This pack train left no tracks, yet I heard it pass on the trail last night. I was awakened by the *arrieros* talking and whistling. They wanted me to know they were there, Don Alfredo. They weren't trying to slip by me with the pack train."

"Ah, you saw ghosts, then. Good. A visit from ghosts usually means you're close to recovering something precious that was lost, or hidden. It means you're near an *alcancía*, a precious store. You're on the right track, so don't sleep too soundly."

"I was afraid you would want me to believe something like that."

"I'm not asking you to believe it, and don't ask me if I believe it. However, *dicen*—they say—that men see ghosts when they are close to a treasure. Everyone in Sonora knows your Steeldust is a treasure, even the ghosts. Why don't you? It's easy for me to read your dream as a sign that you're close to redeeming your horse, but you don't have to believe it.

"Look, I forbid you to believe it if you think it's a sin. Remember, the pack train was your dream, not mine. What are you asking *me* to believe? You're the one looking for the treasure, not me. The sign was given you, not me."

"This was no dream. I heard the men and animals, saw the sparks off the horseshoes."

"There you are. You answer your own questions. Only ghosts manifest themselves that way. It means good spirits are rallying to help you. Be sure, Bill, that wherever Lindano rides, wherever he camps, no one, ghost or Christian, will whistle or sing as a courtesy to him. Lindano is a leper to us. Every step he takes is marked and remembered.

"We support you in your trouble, though we didn't ask for it. You have friends here because you are good. We know you won't stay here. Whatever happens, you and your horse will be gone when the trouble is over.

"However, do you know how precious that horse is to us who still use the horse as a measure of good? You'll leave here with Steeldust because we are good people. We'll stay on the edge of your fight to assure the horse's safety. We'll stay out of it to make Lindano feel he's safe here. When we go for his throat, he'll be smiling at us."

"Why haven't the people already put an end to him?"

"Hah, the devil wears horns, not a halo. Who wants to go in over the horn to stop him? If we leave him to himself, he'll start the fight that will finish him. You'll see. We have time. Now, thank God, you're here.

"Now, strip to the waist so my woman can start your cure. She has the touch. I'll go out and lead Lizard and the mule to shelter."

Doña Elena splashed mescal on Bill's back and began to knead a sore spot on his spine. She worked his spine between her thumbs. Suddenly, a whole segment of Bill's backbone moved over like a sore man sliding into bed. Then, she massaged Bill's wounded shoulder carefully and tenderly with mescal and salve. Gradually, she worked down the arm to Bill's smashed hand. She kneaded and soaked the fingers in mescal until she had them separated and unclenched from the knot of pain in the center of the hand. She determined the damage they had suffered and relaxed them into their normal places. Bill had been walking around with his hand clenched like a dead chicken's foot since Lindano dropped the rock on it.

Doña Elena packed each finger individually in a fibrous mash ground from the pulp of mescal. She wrapped the hand firmly in cotton cloth so only the tips of Bill's fingers showed outside the pack. The mash began to set like a cast, but was not rigid. The warmth of the hand kept it pliable.

"Now," said Doña Elena. "You can go on about your business for a while. I want you to stay here so I can doctor you every other day. Do not deliver blows in anger or blows that kill. If you kill nothing, not even a fly, with that hand for three weeks, it will heal. Clench nothing. Use it softly and gently, but keep doing your best to use it, and it will heal. I want to keep warm the shoulder and thigh that were wounded. I'll make a down mattress for your bedroll."

Bill was so relieved after the treatment that he slept. Doña Elena covered him with a blanket. In the night, he awoke and saw Don Alfredo sitting by the fireplace.

"Why aren't you resting, *viejo?*" Bill asked.

"I rest by watching the fire and listening to the rain. I was watching you rest. Bill, I wonder if you know how much we love you here. Everyone in the Sierra claims to be your special friend. We worry about this fight. You might get rid of Lindano for us but lose your own life. Whatever happens, we have to take the horse away from him. His fondest ambition is to ride a horse like Steeldust to death. He has reached his peak."

"Don't worry. Steeldust will never carry him a mile. He'll never ride a good horse if he lives a thousand years."

"Maybe you can take the horse he is riding away from him, too."

"I'd never do it. That horse is our best ally. Let the horse he's riding have him. That horse is as mean as Lindano. The farther he goes, the more of Lindano's flesh he exploits, and every once in awhile he'll kick him or wipe the ground with him and make his life pass before his eyes. That horse is as miserable as Lindano. Let them use each other."

"I have to tell you, Bill. You and Steeldust both look bad. Lizard looks like a parade horse compared to Steeldust. We saw him go by. He could not have gone much further. Any horse that has been dunked in the sea and has challenged its vastness to escape a man must have suffered a great shock. Any man who looks into the barrel of a .45 and watches the bullets come to kill him suffers an awful shock. You've been in a decline since you were shot because the *sústo*—the shock of fright—keeps killing until it is alleviated. Food, rest, friendship, love, and caresses are the only cures for you and your horse.

"I once saw a horse fall off the cliff of *Cuchujaqui*. He stumbled on the brink and fell ten meters into the pool. People say this pool, called the pool of the mercury, is bottomless. We thought it had saved the horse, but when he drifted to the surface he was not swimming. He rolled over on his side and drowned. I believe horses who suffer immersion cast themselves away from the limits of their bodies. They do this because they cannot immediately see the best way to save themselves inside the water. When your horse went by here, he was ready to lie down and die. He is suffering the same decline that you are. You will be leaving your body behind more and more while you are obsessed with redeeming your horse.

"Your body is dying and no longer is able to keep up with you. That's the reason you do not recognize old friends on the trail, the reason you have been too hard on your animals. Flesh cannot keep pace with your spirit."

"Other horses might die of *susto* from being dunked in water over their heads," Bill said. "Not my horse. La Jineta swam with him in the Mayo for fun before he tried to escape Lindano by swimming across the sea. He was not afraid of water."

The sound of Don Alfredo's voice began to soothe Bill like a drug. He knew all his *sustos* would go away if he was just given one more chance to get his horse back.

Don Alfredo was droning on about the rain. Bill slept. The rain stopped before he awoke two days later. He stayed in the house another week.

Bill used Don Alfredo's ranch as a hub and began searching the country for Steeldust. His system was to ride out one whole day, make camp and stay overnight, then search different country on his way back to the ranch the next day.

One night he was on the Arroyo de Cuchujaqui in a steep canyon that was fat with game and wild with predators and running water. He camped under a cliff on a clean sandbar by the stream. He was tired. He hid Lizard in the brush and ate a meager, early supper. At midnight, his fire was out and he was sleeping.

He awoke when he heard a horseman approaching his camp on his side of the canyon. The trail was on the other side. Bill's side was choked with boulders and brush, a hard place to ride a horse in the daytime, impossible at night. The horseman was singing in a fine, clear baritone to alert Bill's camp. The steady, shod hoofbeats of the horse pounded the rock without faltering as the horseman came on.

Bill was lying in the only path the rider could take to cross the sandbar. Suddenly, he felt the horse's footfall through the ground and realized the horseman was on him and about to prance right over the top of him. Out from under his tarp he came, tangling in his blanket as he tumbled underneath the horse. The horse flounced on over his head. The horseman sang on, sounding amused, but bound to keep on singing and riding and keeping his course. He was gone before Bill could free himself of his tarp and blankets.

Bill sat up and laughed at the thumps his heart was making against his chest. He could not say he had seen the horseman, but he knew the man was about his own age, his own size, and having a good time. In the morning, Bill found no tracks or signs of his visitor.

After that night, Bill scattered gravel in his bed before lying down at bedtime so he would not sleep too soundly. He wanted to be sure he awakened in time to see the next man who rode a horse across his bed. He did not mind ghosts, but if he was close to Steeldust, the next man he met might be Lindano.

A few nights later, while he was sleeping with his tarp over his head, a horse scattered rocks off the hill above him and trotted down to water in the spring where Bill was camped. Bill heard him take the long sips and deep swallows of a thirsty horse. Then he popped and flapped his lips over the surface of the water, playing, like Steeldust often did. He moved away from the stream, walked in a circle, and collapsed on the ground, rolling and grunting. He rubbed his hide in the dirt, stood up, snorted, and shook himself. He paused, then grunted as he relieved himself upon the ground. He walked away toward Lizard and the mule. Bill heard Lizard's soft whiffle. Sleep was heavy as dope on Bill and he could not raise himself.

Bill thought, It's Steeldust and he's found Lizard. I've got him. He'll stay with Lizard. If I jump up and try to catch him in the dark, I'll just run him off. If he goes away, I'll track him in the morning.

At first light, Bill looked out and did not see the horse. He went to fill his coffee pot at the spot the horse had watered. He was sure this time he would find the sign, but the horse had left no sign, no wallow in the earth where he had rolled, nothing.

A week later, Bill was searching down the Mayo river toward the flats of Mocuzari. He made an early camp under big alamo trees. He had seen and talked to no one but Lizard all day. He was a day's ride back in the direction of Chihuahuita. He had his mule and provisions with him. He hung his panniers and food in a tree.

He awoke in the middle of the night holding his breath. His canvas panniers were being dragged over the ground. The thieves were speaking in low voices, in sharply accented Spanish. The voices belonged to Spaniards, *Gachupines.* He knew the accent. They had to be small men. If they were big men, they would not have to drag the panniers. Spaniards were small. One of the men had a deep, bass voice he could not hush. The other spoke quietly in a gentle voice. Bill could not understand a word they were saying. He lay still and held his breath to see if he could understand them. He could not shoot them. His pistol was in a pannier. He heard spur rowels dragging the ground. He pulled on his boots, picked up a dead limb, squalled, and ran toward a figure under a tree. He lit up the inside of his head with white lights when he collided with his panniers on the way. He sat on the ground and listened to the grind and creak of the manila rope that held the swinging panniers. He stood and hefted his provisions on their swing and knew they were hanging in the same place he had hoisted them before he went to bed.

He rode back to Cochibampo the next day. He was light-hearted. He was sure Steeldust could not be more than one day's ride from Don Alfredo's ranch. He decided he would make his headquarters at the spring of Bacajaqui where the ghost horse had rolled. Maybe that horse had been Steeldust's spirit looking for company. Steeldust must be close to Bacajaqui.

Don Alfredo laughed when Bill told him about the ghostly Spaniards who had tried to steal the panniers. He told Bill to trust his instinct, he had nothing to lose. He should stay in the region and search more closely. Steeldust had been too weak to leave the region.

The next day Bill found himself on the ridge above Ojo de Agua. He passed a spot where he could have seen Steeldust lying by the pool, but he turned his head and missed him. A moment later he looked down at the dark blue eye of the pool and the branches of the *chapote* that were hiding Steeldust. Lizard knew he was there, but Lizard was tending to business and would not nicker to him. Lizard knew that Bill hated a lovesick, nickering horse.

Bill rode on, thinking he had seen the bottom of the canyon well enough. He was sweating with fever and was being rained on again. He wanted to ride back to his camp and wait for the rain to subside.

He rode down by the entrance of the canyon and saw Lindano's barricade. He dismounted and tore away the brush pile and led Lizard to the *chapote,* intending to take shelter.

He noticed that the last nubbin of browse and grass had been eaten in Ojo de Agua, along with most of the bark of the small trees and brush. He dropped Lizard's reins and walked away from the *chapote* and saw Steeldust lying in a swale, his tail and mane fanned out on the ground, his body flat against it, as though he had tendered his carcass for death. Bill's heart began aching so much he dropped to his knees. The horse was dead, or awfully sick. He could not be healthy if he was sleeping so hard he was unaware of Bill and Lizard. Not a hair moved on him, not a breath swelled his sides.

Bill whistled to him, the same as he had whistled to him all of his days. Steeldust moved an ear. Again, Bill whistled the call he had always used for Steeldust. The beginnings of a whiffle quivered in the horse's nostrils, but he still did not awaken. Bill walked toward him and kept whistling and the horse whiffled plainly in his sleep. Bill smiled.

"Come on, old feller. Come on, old man, time to go home," Bill said.

Steeldust raised his head off the ground, eyes closed, still sound asleep, and nickered to Bill. Bill touched him and he opened his eyes and stood up. Bill ground his knuckles into his eyes, sat down, and wept like a boy.

As soon as he could see, Bill studied the horse. He was thin, frail, starved, but his hide and hair were healthy. Both his eyes were clear and his look was untroubled, though a cloud the size of a pinhead dotted the corner of his left eye.

Bill led Steeldust and Lizard out of Ojo de Agua and the horse walked companionably at his shoulder, his breath always close on Bill's shirt. Outside the canyon, Bill stayed on foot and led the horses toward Don Alfredo's ranch. He did not need to ride and hurry away to look for a better place. He had found his horse, and he felt they should celebrate and go slow. He let Steeldust and Lizard graze on the way back to Cochibampo.

Don Alfredo put Lizard and Steeldust away with plenty of corn and *tasol*. Bill was so tired Don Alfredo had to help him to the house. Bill stayed and rested and helped Don Alfredo in the peace and quiet of the ranch while Steeldust improved. The horse had been saved by the browse in the canyon and by his willingness to rustle for every leaf and blade he could reach, by his great, calm heart, and by the grace of God. Bill watched and saw that every bite he ate counted, and he began to grow stronger. Bill worried about him though, because he slept all the time and would not eat from Bill's hand. When he was not eating, he was content to stand himself by Lizard's side and sleep.

"Don't worry about that," Don Alfredo told Bill. "He has to come back slowly from the place where he stored his soul so it would not leave him. He has to go back there often so he can control his recuperation. It rests him. He is a smart horse. He knows if he does not control his appetite, he will die. He also has to make sure you are still a good man. For all he knows, you might take him to another canyon to beat and starve him. Allow him to moderate his appetite and find his dependence on you again. You have to admit, lately, you have not been a good provider for him."

"He won't eat until I've set his feed down or hung his *morral* over his ears. He won't eat out of my hand," said Bill. "He doesn't notice me when I pet him."

"Were you in the habit of petting him before?"

"Never. I rubbed him but never got familiar with him. He never petted me, either. We got along."

"Then, don't condescend to him now. You are his partner. Give him the *pinchi* alone. My wife and I will give him his *caricias,* his caresses."

Bill stopped bothering the horse, and Steeldust's strength seemed to grow faster. Bill's strength did not grow. He could not shake the fever. The horse grew healthier than he, and Doña Elena kept fussing over him, unhappy with his progress.

After three weeks, Bill quit trying to convalesce and began riding Steeldust again. The horse looked better under the saddle. Standing in the corral, hipshot, he looked like an old plug. Under the saddle, his pride and dignity awakened, he became the personable stud again. Bill rode him on short jaunts and visited his friends in the Sierra. Lindano's name was never mentioned anywhere. Bill rode to Alamos and sent a wire to Pascual, telling him he had recovered the horse. On the day before he was to start back to Chihuahuita an answer came from Pascual:

> *Lindano seen between you and me at Mocuzari.*
> *Wait for me there on the first day of the fiesta.*

"Your horse and your girl are safe now, Bill," Don Alfredo told him. "My God, your lives have been returned to you.

Don't go to Mocuzari. Go to Chihuahuita for María, load her and your horses on the train, and go home. Leave Lindano to stew in his own meanness."

"I am going home. Mocuzari's on my way. The fiesta of San Alberto will be going on. Why don't you come with me? Your neighbors will all be there."

"It's only a *jaripeo,* a horseman's festival."

"I like the *jaripeo.* I'll be well mounted."

"Then, ride Lizard and leave Steeldust here. Come back for him after the trouble. Why endanger him again?"

"Steeldust goes with me to Mocuzari and from there to Chihuahuita, and from there to Arizona. I have him so I can be horseback and he's my top horse."

Bill saddled Lizard, packed the mule, tied Steeldust's lead to the mule's tail, and rode toward Mocuzari. He rode through Los Tanques and La Vinata. The children ran ahead and announced his horse wherever he went. The whole country was packing and loading wagons to go to the fiesta at Mocuzari.

Bill felt so unwell he just sat up on Lizard and trusted the people to warn him if Lindano was near. He knew he was too slow, crippled, and crazy for a man-to-man fight, but he had to face the final trouble. If Lindano ran, or did not run, the matter would be finished.

The fiesta had begun when he rode into Mocuzari. He rode the length of the main street enjoying the music. He stopped at the corral of his friend, Manuel Velderrain, who owned a mercantile store. Manuel ordered his sons to unsaddle, feed, and water Bill's animals. He led Bill into a cool storeroom he had emptied of wares and furnished with a bar and tables for the fiesta.

Bill sat at a window and rested where he could watch his horses. He was feverish and he began drinking mescal. Friends came to greet him. They talked a short while and then left him alone. Others came, talked about his feud with Lindano and went away. Bill soon realized why no one would stay and drink with him. People were coming to the fiesta of Mocuzari that year to watch a killing. The people were on his side, but none were coming to prevent the fight. Bill's friends did not want to sit and drink with him long because he was the target of the meanest man they knew. No one expected Bill to give up his horse unless he was dead. Bill was in Mocuzari, so he must be there looking for Lindano to get even with him. The people were happy about this and prepared to enjoy the fight. Bill was not against the fight at all, but he wondered if anyone had thought to sell tickets. Even Pascual had made sure Bill would be there to have it out with Lindano.

A group of musicians walked in singing a *corrido* (a ranch ballad) about Steeldust, La Jineta, El Mostrenco and Lindano: the stallion, the headlong girl, the maverick named Bill, and the man Lindano they called the Gila monster. Every musician in town knew the song and had come to watch Bill and Lindano write the ending.

Fever, exhaustion, pain, and mescal had finally subdued Bill. No one else knew it, but Bill was finished. He shook hands with old friends but did not know them. Pascual, Placido, and Mary rode in and left their horses in the corral with Lizard and Steeldust. Bill watched them but did not know them. He did not rise to hug Mary when she came in, and when she saw the state he was in she stayed away from him. He smiled at Pascual and shook his hand and thought he probably would soon remember his name. Mary looked just like any other Mayo Indian or Yaqui boy.

Mary and Pascual sat by Bill, and all of a sudden his pain left him and his mind awakened. He looked around and no one was bothering with him anymore. He moved across the room and nobody spoke to him. He could rise above the people, or stand among them, as he wished. He could read every face in the room at once in detail, no matter how far away they were or which way they were turned. He knew all their names and all their concerns. Mary was the only female in the room. She was sitting as close under Pascual's shoulder as she could be, listening and watching everything. She showed little expression and no awareness that the people were coming into the room and flocking to the windows to admire her.

Bill saw himself sitting by the window asleep. He stared at the big lump of his body, with sweat making a pool at its throat, and was sorry he was leaving it. He was thankful it was no longer in pain, but he felt he had let it down by leaving it before it was altogether used up.

A group of ladies came in, smiling and apologizing. They went to Mary like sister hens and politely ordered her to go with them. She stood up and looked back at Pascual.

"Go," Pascual said. "I'll have Bill ready when you are. We'll bring your horse when you're dressed."

Mary turned and looked at Bill's hulk by the window.

"He's asleep," Pascual said. "We'll let him rest awhile."

Mary went out with the women. Bill looked down at his flesh and thought he better crawl back into his poor shell and see if he could get it to moving again. He decided he felt too good the way he was, and he wanted to see if he could go out into the street. Pascual was laughing with Manuel and taking his first drink of mescal. Bill wished Pascual would stop him from leaving. He knew each step he took away from his body now would make it harder for him to return.

A rooster-pull was being held in the street. A rooster had been buried to his neck. The contestants ran their horses by him, hung from their saddles, and snatched at his head as they went by. Bill stood by the poor old rooster. Placido came rattling down the street on his paint mare with a wild grin on his face, scratched the ground with his fingers, and scooped up the rooster. The rooster gasped, as though this was even a worse fate than he had expected. Placido regained his seat and waved him over his head. The mare ran to the end of the street. *Vaqueros* who had tried for the rooster and missed ganged up in good humor and rushed Placido to take it away from him. The whole mob ran back down the street with Placido laughing in the lead.

A man on a black horse barreled into the street and collided with Placido's mare. He snatched the rooster away from Placido, screamed in triumph, and raced away, wringing the chicken's neck over his head. The body tore loose, bounced, and beat its wings at the feet of a pride of musicians, scattering them. The man was Lindano. Copper had turned jet-black. Placido and the other contestants left the street. Lindano held up the rooster's head and spurred Copper into a frenzied dance. The rooster's head flopped back and forth across his knuckles in time with the music, and the musicians began composing new stanzas of the *corrido* of Steeldust.

Bill looked into the faces of the people. They were hiding their disapproval of Lindano but showing their faces to him. They were patient to witness his finish. They would enjoy it more if he did more to condemn himself.

Copper danced beautifully, his neck arched, his feet tapping the hard street. He probably would not survive this abuse by Lindano. The day would be long with many songs to be danced. Lindano ordered the musicians to follow him as Copper pranced along. A crowd fell in behind the horse and the musicians. Copper was so agitated he would probably founder or die of heat stroke. Lindano was wearing his big spurs with the hobbled rowels, and he kept raking Copper's flanks, his face rapt with pleasure. Then his eye fell on Steeldust.

Steeldust had already seen Lindano. Lindano spurred Copper in a dash for the corral. Someone shouted with excitement and more people ran out and joined the crowd. Placido was standing by the gate and he opened it for Lindano. Lizard, Pascual's and Marco's mules, and other horses were in the corral, but Steeldust was standing by himself in a corner. The crowd rushed for places to watch Lindano and Steeldust.

Steeldust was fully recovered now and alert to defend himself.

All the musicians who had come to the fiesta formed together at the corral and began to play the *"Diana,"* the song of accolade. Lindano took down a maguey rope and began to flower a loop to the tune of the music. He grabbed a bottle of mescal out of his morral, turned it up to drink from it, and made the stuff burst and gurgle inside the bottle while he kept his loop open. He dropped a loop over Steeldust's head and spun it off before it closed. Bill wished he had his pistol, but he had left it somewhere out of reach again. Lindano rolled a loop over Steeldust's hips and it made a trap in front of his hind legs. Steeldust did not step into the loop, so Lindano picked it up, spun it flatly in front of his horse, brought it behind him, and let it whip into Steeldust's rump. The crowd laughed as Steeldust kicked up primly at the rope. He whirled to face Lindano and the crowd hooted at him for being goosy.

Lindano tried to circle Steeldust to get behind him again, but the horse shuffled away to stand inside the crowd of the other horses. Lindano rushed at them and started them running around the corral. Then he stood Copper in the center and pressed the others against the fence, waiting for a throw at Steeldust. Steeldust kept the other horses and mules between himself and Lindano as they ran.

Lindano ran in behind Steeldust, beat him over the rump with his loop, and drove him toward the gate. "Open the gate, open it," he commanded, but Placido was on the gate and he only grinned at Lindano. Steeldust cut back at the gate, and Copper went on by and ran into the gate with his chest. Steeldust joined the bunch again and watched Lindano beat Copper between the ears with the double of his rope. Lindano finally tired of beating his horse, looked up, and spurred Copper at Steeldust again. Copper, cold-jawed, careened through the bunch and scattered it.

Bill wished someone would shoot Lindano, but the people were laughing and enjoying the show. Bill stepped through the fence and walked into the corral. The horses and mules had bunched together again. Bill looked for a big rock so he could knock Lindano off his horse but found none big enough.

Lindano spurred Copper toward Bill. Bill stepped aside, and Copper went on by and split the bunch in two. Lizard flushed away with half the bunch and left Steeldust behind. Copper bounced off the fence, reared, lunged, and loosened Lindano's seat. Steeldust saw a lane of daylight between Copper and the fence and powered through to catch up to Lizard. Lindano threw away his rope so he could grapple with his saddlehorn and accidently spread his loop over Steeldust's head as he ran by. The coils of the rope were lying over the saddlehorn and they looped on Lindano's wrist. Steeldust hit the end of the rope and caught Lindano's hand fast against the saddlehorn, nearly severing it at the wrist and binding Lindano to his horse. Copper was jerked down to his knees, and he straddled the rope with his hind legs when he stood up again. Lindano's saddle slipped to Copper's side. Copper gave himself to the devil and pitched around the corral with the rope between his hind legs and Steeldust running wild on the end, keeping it tight.

Copper and Steeldust bracketed all the horses and mules in the corral between them. Lindano was hanging head-down over Copper's side, holding on with a leg and spur hooked over his back. The pack of horses and mules headed for the gate at a dead run. Placido swung it open, let them out, and grinned as they went by.

The pack of horses and mules between Steeldust and Copper jammed Lindano in place so he could not fall and be dragged. The pack stayed tightly together as it raced down the street. Then La Loca, the mule, stumbled and fell

and rolled underfoot. The pack loosened. Lindano lost his
hold and slipped under Copper's belly. Copper went berserk
and pulled Steeldust tightly into the pack again.

The pack yawed and turned back down the street and
headed toward the crowd again with Copper dragging
Lindano and kicking him every jump. The crowd scattered
and as the pack ran by, Bill saw the man's head was being
scalped and flayed by rock and hoof. The body was limp as
a wet hide and was caught in the wind of the stampede. It
was being buffeted, bumped, jerked, and bounced until
every bone was broken, the toes awry, the face gone.

The stampede went on and Lindano was dragged through
a cholla field at the end of town. The crowd ran after the
pack and met it as it came back across the field. Bill marveled
at the new and unlucky ways the animals could direct their
panic straight down through their hooves into Lindano's
body.

Then Steeldust and Copper bracketed a tree and stopped,
and the rest of the pack scattered. Lindano was lying between
Copper's hind legs. One of Copper's feet kept up a spasm
of kicking. Each time the hoof struck out, it smashed
Lindano's face again.

The townspeople crowded in to take hold of the horses.
The horses crowded tighter over Lindano, trampling him
more. Steeldust was choking on the rope. A man caught
Copper's bridle, another cut the rope to Steeldust, another
cut the cinch on Lindano's saddle, and it fell clear so
Lindano's body was free of the horse. Nobody even looked
at Copper as he wandered distractedly into the cholla field.
Lindano's body was at Bill's feet.

Bill looked at the tangle of meat and bone heaped in a
batter of blood, earth, and cholla and saw one spot on the
body that was undefiled. Lindano's clean, freshly shaven,
upper lip bore no scar, no blood, no smudge of dirt. Bill
bent over and looked more closely. Lindano was finished,
but he bore no scar that had been caused by Bill, not even

on that upper lip where Bill had hit him with his spurs. Bill turned away toward Manuel Velderrain's corrals.

"Now, what about me?" Bill asked himself. He knew no one could hear him. "What's to become of me?" He was almost positive he had lost his mortal place on earth.

He looked to his own bones slumped by the window of the storeroom. Everybody thought he was just sleeping. Pascual was standing near a man and a woman who were sitting on their horses by the corral. Bill knew those people better than he knew anyone else in the world. The cowman on the big, roan horse was his father. The lady sitting sidesaddle on Sam, the stocky bay horse, was his mother. She smiled quickly at Bill, as though she had been waiting for him to notice her. Bill's father looked at him in the speculative way he always first looked at his stock when he had been away, gauging his condition, seeing in an instant how well Bill had been during his absence.

Bill's father was holding Steeldust. The couple rode toward him leading his horse. Steeldust was saddled with Bill's saddle. His mother kept smiling at him and when she was close she stopped smiling and he saw she had tears in her eyes.

"We had come for your wedding, Son," she whispered.

Steeldust was freshly brushed and groomed. The last time Bill had seen him he had been choking on the end of Lindano's rope.

"Get on him, son," said William Henry Shane Sr., offering Steeldust's reins. "He sure made a good horse. I like him."

Bill took the reins and felt the brush of his father's calloused thumb. He stepped around to mount and felt his mother's soft hand brush the back of his neck the way she liked to do, as though to see if it was still in place, he risked breaking it so much.

"Mary's a fine girl," Bill heard Natalia Shane say. "You were awfully lucky, Son."

"Lucky? You mean until now, Mother?" asked Bill. He

realized, whether he wanted to or not, he would have to ride away with his parents. That was death. When it happened a man had to go. He put his foot in the stirrup to mount his horse, but before he stepped aboard, Mary's voice was in his ear.

"Bill . . . Bill," Mary said. Bill awoke by the window with his face in Mary's hands. He straightened and felt refreshed. A crowd stood around him. Pascual was behind Mary looking worried.

"Thank God," Mary said. "We thought you were dead."

Bill felt so good that he leaned back against the wall and closed his eyes. Maybe he should go and ride a ways with his folks, now that he knew he could come back.

"*No*. Come on, now, Bill," Mary said. Afraid, she began shaking him. "No, you don't."

Bill opened his eyes and grinned at her.

"Now, don't do that again," Mary said. "You're scaring us. You don't even breathe when you do that."

Mary was wearing a pretty dress. Her brown face was scrubbed clean, her black hair shining. Her eyes were blue as blue could be.

"Lindano?" Bill asked.

"Man, where have you been?" Mary asked. "His horse dragged him to death right outside your window."

Bill smiled. He knew. "Now, what? What're you all dolled up for? You getting married?"

"Were you really asleep, or just faking, you big phony?"

"I was taking a rest so I could be fresh for the celebration."

"Well, it's time. You feel like getting ready? Come on, we're going to do it on horseback. Your horse is all brushed and ready."

Later, when Bill was riding his horse, Lizard, down the street toward the church with Mary, and the mariachis were accompanying them on both sides, he looked closely at the sidesaddle Mary was riding on her horse, Steeldust. He knew he was still a long way from being right in the head, but he could almost bet the saddle was the same one his mother had ridden in her day. All those things had stayed with him: one God, one country, one horse, one woman. One mother and father too.

If you have enjoyed this book and would like to receive details of other Walker Western titles, please write to:

Western Editor
Walker and Company
720 Fifth Avenue
New York, NY 10019